Shine

Also by Candy Gourlay

Tall Story

Shine

CANDY GOURLAY

David Fickling Books

OXFORD · NEW YORK

31 Beaumont Street
Oxford OX1 2NP, UK

SHINE
A DAVID FICKLING BOOK 978 0 385 61920 2

Published in Great Britain by David Fickling Books,
a division of Random House Children's Publishers UK
A Random House Group Company

This edition published 2013

1 3 5 7 9 10 8 6 4 2

The Random House Group Limited supports the Forest Stewardship Council® (FSC®),
the leading international forest-certification organisation. Our books carrying the FSC label
are printed on FSC®-certified paper. FSC is the only forest-certification scheme supported
by the leading environmental organisations, including Greenpeace. Our paper procurement
policy can be found at www.randomhouse.co.uk/environment

MIX
Paper from
responsible sources
FSC® C016897

Set in 12/16pt Goudy Old Style

DAVID FICKLING BOOKS
31 Beaumont Street, Oxford, OX1 2NP

www.randomhousechildrens.co.uk
www.totallyrandombooks.co.uk
www.randomhouse.co.uk

Addresses for companies within The Random House Group Limited can be found at:
www.randomhouse.co.uk/offices.htm

THE RANDOM HOUSE GROUP Limited Reg. No. 954009

A CIP catalogue record for this book is available from the British Library.

Printed and bound in Great Britain by Clays Ltd, St Ives plc

To Cynthia Lopez Quimpo
I love you, Mom

1

'Are you listening, Rosa?'

I stared at Yaya. Her eyebrows were knitted on her yellow forehead and her face was suddenly smaller, her eyes hard and burning like black coals.

'Listen, listen. This is important.' The seriousness of her voice and the smallness of her face made me feel suddenly scared. I climbed up onto her lap.

'Imagine what it would be like if the rain stopped,' she said in a hushed voice. 'No more hammering on the rooftops. No more *drip drip drip*. No more *splish splash*, I am taking a bath. Can you imagine it?'

I tried to imagine it, really I did, screwing my eyes shut so that I couldn't see the rain steadily drawing stripes on the window pane. But I couldn't. How could I when here on Mirasol it rained all the time?

All the time. Buckets. Sure, sometimes it was just a wetness in the air that left your hair damp. But often it was a torrent. And then the sea turned into a beast with waves for claws.

'Do you ever wonder, Rosa,' Yaya whispered. 'Do you ever wonder what it would be like if the rain suddenly *stopped*?'

Think, Rosa, think! All the wet sounds suddenly silent, just like that. Like God pressed the wrong button on his remote control. OFF.

The quiet would be instant, wouldn't it? Big. Heavy like a giant's blanket.

That was what it was like that day, Rosa. One moment the weather hissing in your ear, the next, *boom*. Nothing.

People froze, their heads tilted to one side, their ears cupped, waiting for the pitter patter to start again. But it didn't.

They rushed out of their houses, staring up at the heavens. And then they were all talking at the same time, pointing. *Look! Look at the sky! And oh, the clouds!* They were peeling away like old, dry scabs.

And before you knew it, there was just a big blue sheet high above their heads. So blue that everyone found themselves rubbing their eyes. It burned. Who would've thought a colour could do that?

And then the sun came out, a blazing white coin – and there was a smell ... everyone pointed their noses at the sun, like this. *Sniff. Sniff.* What was that strange odour? It was the smell of fire. Oh, yes.

On their faces, on their bare arms and legs, they felt a strange sensation. Like the jabs of a thousand tiny beaks. There was a prickling on their scalps, and from the tops of their heads popped beads of scratchy sweat.

The children were the first to move. No rain to keep them indoors! No need to wear itchy plastic things over their clothes! No rain to crumble their sand castles!

They raced into the streets and down the sandy pathways to the beach, whooping and shouting and ignoring the grown-ups' cries of *Where do you think you're going? BE CAREFUL! Don't go into the sea! It's dangerous!*

The children's joy was like an infection, a happiness virus. And then it was the grown-ups' turn to smile. Everyone startled to hear laughter exploding in their throats. Ha-ha, ha-ha! Everyone was so happy! And they all held their hands up at the sun as if the heat was something you could trap and keep for ever.

Meanwhile.

(Come closer, Rosa, this is the scary part. Here, put your arms round my neck.)

Meanwhile.

Out in the middle of the ocean, a fisherman and his boy sat in a boat, jaws gaping at the flickering sea.

First the waves were grey. Boring. Like porridge with no milk or sugar. Then, abracadabra! They were blue! A blue that kept changing. Dark blue. Light blue. Cobalt blue, Duck-egg blue. Midnight blue. Blue blue. Wow. Wow. Wow.

And then they saw something bobbing on the ocean. What was it? Driftwood? Rubbish? Seaweed?

It was a girl.

Without stopping to think, the boy leaped into the water. It was hard to swim because blue waves are bigger and stronger than grey waves, but he managed to grab her with one arm and swim back. Then with the help of his old daddy he dragged her into the boat.

But too late. She was like a wet rag tangled in their nets, green things in her long, black hair, and no breath on her purple lips.

On her throat there were terrible marks. As if a noose of rope had been tied tight around it.

Burning, angry, puckered.

They decided to take the body to the police. But first, the fisherman said, we must bring her to the priest for a blessing. If we cannot save her body, at least let us save her soul.

At the church, the fisherman went to fetch the priest, leaving his son in the back of their old pickup truck with the body.

The boy stared sadly at the dead girl, at the lashes long and wet on the pale cheeks.

Then her eyelids fluttered. She was alive! The boy leaped to his feet, poised to shout for his daddy.

But when the eyes opened, his voice withered in his throat.

The eyes were so empty and hopeless the boy shivered, as if he'd fallen into a cold hole.

And then the pretty lips parted and the girl began to take long, thirsty gulps of air.

As she drank from the atmosphere, the boy felt his own throat become tighter, the tubes that fed his lungs began to narrow, and soon he too began to gulp. But unlike the girl, whose lips and skin became rosier as she breathed, he opened and closed his mouth, swallowing. To no avail.

Slowly his lungs shrivelled into stones.

The girl watched, her face expressionless as he fell

to his knees, suffocating. Then she whirled and leaped from the truck.

When the fisherman and the priest emerged from the church, the rain had begun to fall again.

The boy lay dead in the back of the truck, and the girl was gone.

Yaya held me close. 'Everyone said the girl was a monster come down from the heavens to make trouble.'

I squirmed on Yaya's lap, incredulous. Was it true?

'It's absolutely true,' Yaya said. 'That's why here on Mirasol we are always afraid. We are always looking over our shoulders for monsters that might steal the life from us. This is our lot. Rain. Every day. And fear.' Yaya pressed her cheek against mine. 'It's important that you know this story, Rosa, no matter what your daddy says. This is why you must hide away . . . and keep anyone from seeing these.'

And her fingers traced the marks that circled my neck.

Burning, angry, puckered.

It was many years later when I found the slogan on the Internet. Liked it so much I printed it out and stuck it up above my desk in the attic with Blu-Tack.

The moment Father saw it he swept it off the wall as if it was a disgusting cockroach.

'ROSA!' he yelled, boiling mad. 'HOW MANY TIMES DO I HAVE TO TELL YOU YOU ARE *NOT NOT NOT* A MONSTER?'

I knew Father would hate it, but I didn't expect him to be that dramatic. Instinctively I moved to the window, in case after all these years he decided that today would be the day to do something about the candles I lit for Mother. That he would throw them out the window, once and for all.

Then he yelled for Yaya. She appeared instantly, as if she'd been standing outside the door the whole time. He glared at her so hard I half expected laser beams to shoot out of his eyes. 'See, Yaya? See?' he ranted, waving the sign around. 'See what your stories do?'

To be fair, Yaya's storytelling really was something else: the kind that required blinds drawn, lights switched off and flashlights shining under sheets. It drove Father mad.

'These are horror stories, Yaya, you'll give the child nightmares,' he used to warn her when I was very little. 'Can't you tell her stories that end in happily ever after?'

But Yaya just looked blankly at him. 'I don't know any stories like that. Why don't *you* go ahead and tell her?'

Father had tried. The problem was, he couldn't tell stories like Yaya did. His voice was a monotone, his accent clipped and he didn't bother with sound effects – didn't so much as moan or groan, bare his teeth or flap the sheets.

Right now Yaya just smirked up at him with unblinking eyes. '*Stories?* They're not just stories. They're true. Anyway Rosa can make up her own mind. She's thirteen years old already!'

Father ground his teeth together and the scraping of them put my own teeth on edge. He turned to me. 'Rosa, Mother had it too. Would you call *her* a monster?'

'Monster is what monster does,' Yaya said, her philosophical face on.

Fine. We were all agreed. I was not a monster. Neither was Mother.

But here are the facts:

The marks are there. Round the base of my throat. Unambiguously, inescapably, unmistakeably right *there*.

They are ugly thickenings the texture of rope. See the puckers, the shrivelled folds, the welts. Like burn scars . . . except these were scars acquired not from some fiery accident but deep in the womb before I was born.

And last but not least – deep in my throat, under the hideous scars – the mechanisms that form words and shape sounds are withered and useless.

I cannot speak. All I can manage is an animal '*ungh ungh ungh.*' Not attractive. Probably quite monster-like as a matter of fact.

I've communicated in sign language since I was born, my hands fluttering like birds and shaping words in the air, but when I'm not thinking the noises still escape from my throat. '*Ungh ungh ungh!*' Horrible.

Mother had IT and I've got IT . . . and IT is called the Calm.

It's got a proper medical name, of course, something long, unpronounceable, forgettable. It's incurable – but no, it's not life-threatening, as long as you take the right precautions.

Did I mention that Father's a doctor? A doctor of the Calm, to be precise. Which is no coincidence, because how else did he meet Mother? But more of that later.

There were dangers, of course. There were drugs to be taken every day to keep everything level. Miss one element of the drug cocktail and there were horrible attacks – Father installed a first-aid kit in the bathroom just in case, complete with injections in case I seized up and fell over.

We even practised with a dummy injector, with Father hovering and instructing in a patient voice. *Go on, Yaya, stab it into her thigh, you'll have to do it right through the fabric of her trousers. Then wait ten seconds. Count the seconds in elephants! One elephant, two elephant, three elephant.*

So, yeah. All precautions were taken. No big deal.

But I felt so well! I couldn't speak, yes, but that was just part of our everyday, that was our normal.

Sometimes I wondered if the Calm was just a medical fantasy. In all my thirteen years I have yet to use the kit, yet to experience any attacks, yet to have the emergency injection, even though we've practised a million billion times. Did I really have this terrible, life-threatening condition?

I had to look in the mirror, see the hideous marks, to remind myself the Calm was still there.

Elsewhere in the world, it was no big deal either.

Just another horrible chronic condition. Like horrible Crohn's disease or horrible leprosy or horrible cystic fibrosis or lupus or asthma or Aids. Just another bad thing that couldn't be helped, an act of God . . . life goes on.

But on Mirasol, the Calm was no act of God.

The marks singled me out.

Fingers were pointed and prayers whispered. The Calm. She has it. Remember the story? The day the sun shone. It's her, isn't it? Demon. *Monster*.

So, really, in Mirasol the safest thing to do for someone with the Calm was to get out of the way.

Stay inside.

Hide.

When Mother and Father moved from London to the island all those years ago, they knew how things were, of course. Mother knew what she was getting into – of course she did; she was born in Mirasol, grew up there. She was no stranger to the superstition and the fear. She'd experienced it first-hand.

And yet it wasn't Father who made the original choice to move to Mirasol. It was Mother.

'I begged Kara to change her mind,' Father always said. 'But she was adamant. Jon, she told me, in England, you are surplus to requirements. In Mirasol

. . . well, there were never ever enough doctors in Mirasol when I was growing up. You would make such a difference. In England, nobody will notice that you're gone.'

So they went.

Would they have gone ahead with the move if they'd realized Mother was pregnant? I often wondered.

By the time they realized I was on the way, it was too late to change their plans. 'You were such a surprise!' Father told me.

But not as big a surprise as when they realized that I too had the Calm.

3

Kat, when I look up at Mount Banawa, I can't help but think. She'd seen us as babes, watched as we grew up. She knew more than we did, I bet. She must have seen everything that happened. And she probably knew how it was all going to turn out.

Kara, you said, *have you ever wondered what it must be like to be a mountain? To be so ancient, to know everyone, to see everything . . .* We were just nine years old when you asked me.

And we both gazed up at her jungled peak, waterfalls streaming down her slopes, her presence looming over Mirasol.

Whenever we studied the mountain like that, I felt an odd thing coiling in my gut that was both comforting and alarming at the same time. A spooky feeling. Because it was true about Banawa knowing everything, wasn't it?

She must have known we were special, you and I . . . mirror twins, each the reflection of the other. Kat and Kara. Kara and Kat.

Whenever I looked at you, it was like staring into an enchanted looking glass.

My right eye was a match for your left. I wrote with my left hand while you wrote with your right. Your right foot was one size bigger than your left, and mine was a size bigger than my right.

Remember how Mama used to buy us two pairs of the same shoes, one a size smaller than the other? And how we used to swap lefts for rights? I can't imagine how we would have coped otherwise.

We shared the same bed, didn't we, Kat? We shared a bed until we were in our teens, in fact! We slept face to face, left knee to right knee. When I opened my eyes in the morning, your sleeping face was the first thing I saw.

Mama loved to tell the story of how she used to feel us moving together, deep in her womb. We were like those synchronized swimmers in the Olympics, she said. When one breathed in, the other breathed out. When one kicked, the other kicked too.

I loved to imagine us ripening together in Mama's tummy, face to face, nose to nose, knee to knee. After we were born, Mama said we continued to move synchronously in our cot as if we were still bound together by her womb.

I like to imagine that twins all over the world were just like us sisters, constantly measuring, comparing. But what about the things we couldn't see or measure? Were our souls identical too? Or were they reversals of each other? One dark, the other light? One good, one bad?

Mirror twins. Identical twins, but physically perfect opposites. Well. Perfect apart from the Calm, of course.

What happened there, deep in Mama's womb? And when did it happen? When did the Calm find its way between us sleeping babes? At what point did it choose which one of us to take? At what point did it wrap itself around one infant's throat and release its poison, leaving one unspoiled and the other scarred and mute, its prisoner for ever after?

And so one of us had to stay at home while the other went to school. One of us had to hide, while the other lived in the world. One of us lived in fear while the other had her freedom.

Our parents were teachers. They earned enough for us to live happily. But leaving Mirasol was not an option. Where would we go? What would we do? The world didn't need any more teachers. Not from Mirasol anyway.

But I remember that day you turned to me, eyes shining. We were teenagers by then, wondering how to escape this future.

'Kara! I think I know what we can do!' you said. 'Look, see. Read this article in the newspaper. World nursing shortage. Nurses! Every hospital in the world is desperate for nurses. I can train to become a nurse and get a job in another country. That will be our ticket out of here!'

And it was such an exciting idea. A happily ever after! Who would've thought? All this time we had believed we would always have to live on the island, this dreaming place, so beautiful and yet so filled with a fear of the unknown that I was condemned to hide myself away. If Kara became a nurse she could take me with her to another place, a country that didn't see evil in the shadows, or monsters in the scars on a little girl's throat. We wouldn't need to continue living with this injustice: one sister in the dark and the other in the light.

Night after night, we lay awake planning how we would live, how we would travel, away, away! The house we would live in. The colours we would paint the rooms, what furniture we would buy; the holidays we would have in exotic places, the cars we would learn to drive, the dinners we would cook for each other. We would find husbands and have babies. And our babies would grow up together and we would do a big dinner every Sunday, us cooking together all day while our families played games and laughed and talked.

It was a simple dream. A simple idea of a simple future. A life.

And you were so sure, Kat, weren't you, that we could make it come true?

Well, not we. You.

Only you could go out there, train as a nurse. Only you could get that job in another country. Only you, Kat. It had to be you.

As always.

4

The moment Father stomped off to his study I retrieved the Monster poster from the bin.

Yaya shook her head and whistled softly. 'I don't know what's got into your coconut, Rosa. You know how sensitive Doc is about the Calm and your mother. Mam Kara is always in his head.'

I shrugged. Sure, but why did he have to be sensitive on *my* behalf?

Yaya left, and I sighed as I listened to the slap of her slippers dwindling on the wooden staircase. I smooshed the poster into my desk drawer and slammed it shut.

If Mother were still alive, I'd bet she wouldn't be like Father. So solemn and nervous about everything. I'd bet she would have laughed her head off at that poster and asked me to print her a copy.

I knelt at the window and sorted through the candles on its broad sill. It was probably the bazillionth time I was rearranging them that day, but I didn't care.

I leaned over the sill and peered out the window. The light was lowering. It created a saintly halo on Banawa's crown. On the sea, the rain was shushing softly.

My fingers itched to light the candles. Mother, Mother.

Stop it, Rosa. It's still too light outside. Too early. Wait till sundown. Think of other things.

I made myself get up and sit at my desk. Made myself fire up the laptop, pull up the essay I'd been working on for home school. My hand hovered over the keys but I clenched it away. No! Not now. No Internet! You've got homework, for Banawa's sake! No checking for tweets and comments and likes and . . .

A pink text bubble popped open on the screen.

It floated slowly across my essay to the opposite side, bouncing off the bezel like a rubber ball.

Inside the bubble was a tiny blue witch avatar on a flying broomstick waving her pointy hat like a cowboy. It was Blue Cackle.

My heart sank. Not again. Blue was someone I'd friended only a month ago. Nice enough. But she didn't take the NO LIVE CHAT notice on my profile seriously. Her bubble quivered like it couldn't contain itself.

Stroppyweather!
Ahoy! Ahoy!

Stroppyweather. That was what I called myself online. My avatar was a superhero in a tight leotard with leathery pterodactyl wings flapping from her shoulder blades and a gravity-defying bosom.

There wasn't anything gravity-defying about the real me, of course. But that's the point, isn't it? That's what's so exciting about the Internet. It's not about what's real but about aspiration. About being whatever it is that you want to be.

In Mother's time, anyone unlucky enough to get the Calm ended up hiding away. But now . . . well, this is the age of the Internet, isn't it? In the age of connectedness, there are no longer such things as towers, no Rapunzels – no such thing as alone. You don't have to go looking for a social life, it comes looking for you.

Like right now.

I bit my lip.

Blue's bubble bounced insistently.

> Hello! Hello! Hello!

Two days ago, Blue had emailed me: *Why no live chat, Stroppyweather? I wanna live chat with you!*

I was flattered, of course. But a rule was a rule. I emailed her back: *My dad thinks it's dangerous. If he finds out I'm live chatting he'll ban me from the Internet for sure. Anyway, we're practically live chatting now.*

Well, Father didn't really ban me from live chatting. He wouldn't know a chat from a tweet. But it was easier to blame him than to admit that it was me. Because the truth is, though I was happy to be connected in a quadrillion other ways, chatting in real time just – well, it made me feel exposed.

It was just too . . . instant. There was no time to choose your words, to rehearse a lie; no chance to put on another face. It was too real, too close for comfort. I ran a finger along the twisted skin on my neck. Live chat was one step closer to face to face. And then what would my so-called friends say when they discovered the . . . the *thing* hiding behind Stroppyweather?

Most people just gave up trying to live chat me

after being ignored for the gazillionth time, but Blue had been more persistent than most. I'd lost count of the number of times Blue had tried to draw me in.

She must really like me.

> How's you, girlfriend? Talk to meeeee!

You're lovely, Blue Cackle. I really like you too. But this is the limit.

I sighed and jabbed at the keyboard.

An ominous black box rolled onto the screen.

> You are about to block this person PERMANENTLY. This person will no longer be able to see you or contact you. Do you really want to do this?

I only hesitated for a fraction of a second. Then my index finger landed on the keyboard like a small fist. *Thump.*

Blue Cackle's bubble exploded into particles all over my screen like tiny pink tears.

I suppose our house could pass as a tower. It was tall and thin, with a steep staircase and high ceilings. On the side, like a lumpy wart, was a dilapidated garage for Father's car.

Father and Mother had chosen our home well – it was within easy driving distance of Father's hospital but tucked away on a quiet elbow of Mirasol's southern shore.

There were three other houses on our road but our house turned away from them, as if it had half a mind to leave. The others huddled together on the far end, conspiring.

The nearest clump of civilization was a village twinkling in the far distance. There was a concrete promenade edging the sand that someone had built long ago, complete with ornate street lighting. But the iron of the street lights had long since corroded in the salty air. Ever since I could remember, only one of the lamps had ever managed to light up.

I don't suppose Rapunzel or the Hunchback of Notre Dame had a nice quiet beach to escape to when they were fed up with their respective towers.

Ours was a pretty good one – sand like talcum powder, swaying coconut trees. Paradise, but with weather. I had long stretches of unvisited beach to stroll on, unseen.

One of the reasons Father and Mother had picked the area was because nobody from the village ever ventured to this end of the beach. The surf was too fierce, the rip current notorious.

A small, home-made sign at the end of the promenade shooed people away.

Scribbled down below someone had added some morbid statistics:

UNSEEN CURRENTS HAVE KILLED

IIII IIII IIII I

That was our bit of the sea. Beautiful to look at, dangerous to hold. Lucky for me.

I sat staring at the empty laptop screen for a long time. Sadness pressed down on my shoulders. Oh, Blue. I'm sorry, sorry, sorry.

A normal girl would have gone on live chat without batting an eyelash. But I wasn't normal, was I?

I flicked back to my essay but the words on the screen could have been hieroglyphics. I couldn't get my head to pay attention. My essay was not going to get written today.

Yaya was always telling Father I couldn't be trusted tto police myself online. What an irony!

Last night at dinner, she had such a go at me. 'Pah! They are not real friends, Rosa. They're imaginary! Don't you agree, Doc? Doc?'

But Father, of course, wouldn't be drawn. He just gave her a shifty sideways look, his lips compressed so that dimples appeared on either side of his chin. He *wanted* me to have a social life, didn't he? Why else did he get me a new laptop last year when I turned thirteen?

I had 388 people on my friend list now – 388 souls I had to constantly keep at arm's length. As Blue Cackle just found out, there was a line my so-called friends couldn't cross. Yaya had no idea.

I sighed and stared glumly out the window.

Banawa gazed back at me. The setting sun cast long shadows across the mountain, remoulding one ridge into a nose and turning the broad overhang into a forehead. Deep indentations became eyes and the white streams flowing down shone like tears on the mountain's green cheeks.

There she was, crying again.

Mirasol was long and narrow, a pancake of an

island with the mountain balanced on one end. One of these days I wouldn't be surprised if the whole place teetered over like a playground seesaw, all the sand from the beaches on one side cascading over to the other side.

I heaved another deep sigh, turning to the screen. Idly I typed 'Banawa' and 'Mirasol' into the search.

Immediately the screen filled with thumbnail photos of the mountain.

But oh, the horror of Mirasol photography! It was always like this: blurred, over-exposed or under-exposed, the photos all looked like they'd been snapped by mistake. We were the capital of the world for rubbish snapshot-takers. I sighed.

But then something caught my eye at the top of the thumbnail collection.

I clicked on it and a photograph bloomed across the screen, rich and green.

Oh my.

It was the Banawa I knew and loved, gazing up sadly, the sky swirling with black-soaked clouds, silver falls streaming from her hooded eyes onto the rich green forest of her face. It was beautiful and yet somehow tragic at the same time.

I felt light-headed. And my pulse was roaring, as if

a storm surge had suddenly erupted in my wrists. The photo's composition, the angle of the shot, the way it was framed . . . *it looked as if it had been taken from my window.*

But how could it?

Calm down, girl, look at that angle. Not quite from your window. The angle was from ground level. I frowned. From our front door, then?

Someone had taken the photo from right outside our house.

I clicked through. The photographer used the screen name 'Ansel95'. Below, there was a stream of glowing comments. *Congratulations, nice picture. Excellent light. Perfect. Great composition, well done.* The usual thing.

There was a whole album of photos. Not just of Banawa, but of the rest of the island. I flipped through it, almost forgetting to breathe.

There were twenty-four photographs in all, and every single one was as beautifully composed as the first. But as each photo slid across the screen my heart contracted.

There, in vibrant colour, were images of our road, with the three other houses huddled companionably together. There was the beach, shot right up close, through clumps of sea grass. There was the grey stretch of promenade, swimming with rain puddles. Over a dune I could see the stacked, corrugated iron roofs of the distant village. And finally, there, on the end of our lonely road, was our house, tall and skinny, all its windows shuttered, except for the bright yellow square of the attic window at the very top. My window.

I checked the album's upload date. September the twenty-first. That was just *yesterday*.

I hugged myself tight. Breathe, Rosa. Breathe.

I rushed to the window and threw open the shutters.

Are you out there now?

But all I could see was the deserted road, the ocean beating against the shore and the mountain gazing up at the sky.

I hurried downstairs, snuck out of the front door in my bare feet. I looked carefully up and down our road. No sign of cars or neighbours. I jogged down the path which skirted our house and led to the beach. The sharp gravel soon turned into sand which was wet and sticky between my toes.

It was raining as usual, the drops falling like cold drumming fingers on my head.

I marched right up to the deserted promenade. Stared at the pockmarks made by the rain in the sand. At the driftwood lying like bones in the surf. Stared down the white sweep of the shore to the distant village on its elbow.

The photographs made me feel reckless. Here I'd been, sitting in my tower staring out at the world. And then suddenly it was as if the world had appeared on my doorstep.

Who are you, Ansel95?

Where are you?

But in my head nagged Yaya's disapproving voice. *Are you crazy, girl? Are you looking for trouble?*

So I turned and ran back to the house.

5

OK, so over the next few weeks, I stalked him. I'm not proud of it, but why should I apologize?

Why else would he put his stuff out for everyone to see? He *wanted* to be noticed.

It only took a few clicks to find all Ansel95's profiles online. There are a bazillion things you can learn about someone if you know where to look. All the pieces of the jigsaw were there, you just had to fit them together.

For example, he used the same picture on every profile. Same smiling guy in a necktie, really old, thirty or something. Mister Bland. Mister Anybody. What did that tell me? He had something to hide. That picture was camouflage, I was sure of it. That necktie wasn't him. Why be a necktie when you could be anybody you wanted to be?

He allowed the world to see unimportant things about him. That he liked Stephen King horror films.

That he hated romcoms and musicals. That he didn't watch TV.

He *didn't* talk back. All those likes and comments, and not once did he say thanks. Not once did he engage. Not once did he invite conversation. He was all broadcast and no receive. Definitely someone with something to hide.

He was funny. He always found the most bizarre videos to share: the sleepwalking dog, the strongest baby in the world, the monkey who thought it was human.

But the most important thing I found out about him was this: Ansel95 was *local*. He lived somewhere *nearby*.

I went through his albums, downloaded the best photos and turned them into a screensaver for my laptop. Printed out the one of Banawa and stuck it to the wall, next to the window. It was cool to see the two versions of Banawa side by side, one frozen in the photo, the other – in the window – always changing.

Ansel95 took photos of *everything*.

Every day he posted new pictures, and every day I flicked through them like those stray dogs on the beach, sniffing desperately in the scrub for . . . for something.

And every picture startled me with its familiarity. They were all things I recognized . . . things that I'd actually seen and touched and smelled. All this time, I'd thought I was safe, unreachable, alone in my little tower with my own deserted corner of the beach. But I wasn't.

How many times had Yaya and I strolled past that stand of acacia trees bordering the beach? In Ansel95's photo, they bent away from the wind, arms held high like dancers. And those storm clouds boiling black over the ocean; they were the same ones I saw the other day. I had noted them with a glance, but Ansel95 had frozen them into an angry fresco over a thrashing sea. The photos made me rush to the window and look and look and look.

My stomach ached thinking he was out there. Was he standing outside our door right now? Was he one of those shadows glimmering on the distant beach?

Sometimes, in the photos, there were glimpses of Ansel95 himself – his feet crossed on the sea wall with the sea billowing in the background. Shoes tatty and grubby, oversized canvas skate shoes with a Batman print. The trouser legs were narrow-cut jeans with frayed hems. Boyish feet and boyish legs.

In one picture, you could actually see a bit of the photographer reflected in a mirror. Just the lens and an eyebrow. The eyebrow had a piercing in the shape of a safety pin. *Definitely* not a Mister Anybody.

Most likely that 95 in Ansel95 was a birth year, which was kind of bleagh because using your birth year on your screen name was the sort of boring thing someone like Father or Yaya would do. I somehow expected a lot more from someone with a bad-ass piercing.

BUT it was a good clue. So . . . if he was born in 1995 he was probably sixteen years old.

So I watched him. Downloaded his photos, of course. Followed him around the net. Checked his status updates.

Never, ever commented – what would I have had to say if he commented back? But I did click the like button on his shares. Like. Like. Like. Like. Like.

And the more I followed him the more I liked him. I couldn't help myself.

On Doppelgänger Week, everyone on the social web changed their profile pictures to characters, celebs or movie stars that they considered their doppelgängers. (How could Yaya say the Internet was shrinking my brain? Where else would I have learned that 'doppelgänger' was German for look-alike?)

On the first day, Ansel95 picked Superman. I picked Lois Lane.

On the second day, he picked Luke Skywalker. I picked Princess Leia.

On the third day, he picked Buzz Lightyear. I picked Woody.

On the fourth day a message bubble appeared on my screen.

I knew who'd sent it before I saw its avatar. Bland with a necktie.

Ansel95.

The bubble quivered indignantly and I blanched when I read the message.

YOU'RE STALKING ME.

It wasn't a question.

I chewed my bottom lip. Did I do it on purpose? All that following, all that liking? Was *this* what I was hoping for?

The screen beeped again.

> **You're all over my stuff, Stroppyweather. Who are you?**

I held my breath, my fingers hovering over the keyboard.

Delete him. Block him. Danger danger danger, a voice nagged in my ear. My heart boomed.

Deletedeletedeletedelete.

My fingers clattered on the laptop and my reply bubble appeared, eager, quivering, my avatar grinning.

> **I like your photography.**

NO, ROSA! What are you doing?

But the clamour of questions I was dying to ask him drowned out all good sense. *Who are you? Do you live on my street?* was what I really wanted to know.

There was a long pause. My heart was banging so loudly in my chest I almost didn't hear the beep when another bubble popped up.

Thank you. I guess.

You're welcome.

I bit my lip. Now what? Was he going to switch off, go away, delete *me*?

The seconds inched past.

Then another bubble plopped open on the screen.

So. Do you take pictures too?

Yes! I take pictures! Lots of them! Be anybody you want to be, Rosa! Fake it!

But my fingers had a mind of their own.

No. I don't take them. I look at them.

Oh! It sounded so lame! But honesty was probably a good policy when you wanted to make friends properly.

I shook myself. Make a friend? After all the

avoiding and blocking and deleting, you want to make friends?

The screen beeped again.

> **Heh, how do I know that YOU are not some old weirdo?**

Annoyance flared and my fingers had tapped a reply before I could stop myself.

> **I just like your pictures, OK? SORRY. Shall I stop liking your pictures now?**

Oh God. Where did that come from?

> **Dude, feel free to stalk me. That's what the Internet is for. I LIKE you liking my pictures.**

I was so stunned it was like I'd turned to stone. 'Feel free to stalk me'? This wasn't what I was expecting.

> **You still there, Stroppyweather?**

> **Yeh.**

> **I checked you out too, you know.**

A cold finger ran down my spine. How could I forget that he could look me up just as thoroughly as I could him? My heart was suddenly in my throat, as if Yaya was already standing there looking over my shoulder, crookedly-pencilled eyebrows high on her forehead, finger wagging. *I told you so! The Internet is not safe! You should disconnect!*

> **So now YOU'RE stalking me!!!**

> **Takes one to know one.**

> **And what did you find out?**

I began running through all my social profiles on the net. What did they reveal about me? It was all jokey pretend stuff, wasn't it? I didn't post photographs, so there was no visual evidence to link me to anything. I kept to silly things, jokes, generalities, lists of my likes and dislikes, favourite books, favourite films, favourite songs.

> **Nothing massive. You're an enigma, Stroppyweather.**

I let out a sigh of relief.

He found NOTHING.

So there you have it. Here I was saying Ansel95 was trying to be Mister Anybody when the truth was *I* could be anybody, anywhere. Stroppyweather was a digital dummy. I was Miss Anybody.

The beep of another message pierced the silence in the room.

> **Hey, Stroppy.**

> **Yeah?**

> **I think I figured something out about you.**

> **Oh?**

I tried to sound casual, but I was tense, vigilant.

> **You live in Mirasol.**

For a moment I thought there had been an earthquake. I was suddenly light-headed. Like I was falling. I closed my eyes. He knew where I lived. He KNEW.

Stranger danger, I could hear Yaya hissing in my ear. *Stranger danger*.

> **You do, don't you?**

I gritted my teeth. Right. If he was asking for confirmation then he couldn't be sure, could he? He was guessing. I rubbed my palms together as if I had to warm them, even though it was hot in the room. Took a deep breath before I made my fingers type out a reply.

> Mirasol? Never heard of it. Where on earth is that?

6

We were ten years old when we swapped places.

Oh, Kat, I couldn't believe that we'd waited so long. It was a brilliant plan but you weren't sure, Kat, were you?

How we argued! I said twins in the movies did it all the time. You said the movies were not real life. You said: Miss Emily will know it isn't me. I said: didn't you tell me the other day that Miss Emily was as blind as a bat and not even as smart – that she could barely tell one girl from another in your class.

And then you said: my *friends* would know it wasn't me!

And I looked steadily at you until you had to look away. Your friends didn't know, did they, that there were two of you. They wouldn't suspect a thing.

And then you reached over and tugged my plait in that maddening way that you always do when you think you know better than me.

What about the Calm? you said, smirking. Even if you covered up your neck, the moment you opened your mouth, they would know.

Ah yes. The Calm.

How was I going to spend an entire day at school without revealing that I couldn't speak a word?

It did give me pause.

But only for a few days.

And then I had that idea, and I could tell by the look on your face that it was genius! If we could convince everyone that you'd lost your voice, if we could *both* become mute, then there was nothing to stand in our way.

You couldn't argue because I was right, wasn't I? I could feel your sudden nervousness, your sudden realization that this crackpot idea was not crackpot stuff any more.

So we got the coughing started two weeks before the day of the swap.

As we expected, Mama went into full fuss mode, making us drink disgusting teas the colour of poo. She smeared our necks with thick pastes of aromatic eucalyptus oil, then wrapped Papa's big handkerchiefs round our throats.

She made us both go to bed an extra hour early.

You made faces at me, and several times you wanted to quit, but I begged you not to, promising all the enticements that I could think of: I would give you full access to my watercolours, give you a fifty-fifty share of all my desserts for a week, do your maths homework for a month.

So you hung on.

And when it came time for you to pretend you had lost your voice, you could have won an Oscar for Best Actress.

Mama didn't suspect a thing.

We were all set to forge a fake *To-whom-it-may-concern* note from Mama, but we didn't have to. She wrote one without any prompting: *Kat's laryngitis is bad today, please make sure she avoids using her voice* . . .

So nobody was the wiser when it was you that stayed behind for home school with Mama, and it was I who skipped off to school in your place, dressed in your school uniform, hair tied back exactly like yours, your backpack on my shoulder, neck wrapped in a handkerchief smelling of mentholated eucalyptus oil.

I was full of confidence when Papa dropped me off at the school gates, but when I saw the school yard full of smiling girls in their navy skirts and blue ties I was suddenly overcome with shyness.

You and I had gone over and over your sketch mapping the school, so I found your classroom with no difficulty at all. But I couldn't bring myself to march up to the front of the class and take your seat right under the nose of Miss Emily.

Instead, I found an empty chair in the back row, next to a smiley girl with a straight fringe. Mila was her name, I discovered, when Miss Emily took the register.

Mila was great fun, passing me hilarious notes and drawing funny cartoons of the teachers. At break, we had lunch together.

It was a wonderful day.

When I got home I found you glumly sitting up in bed with a cup of Mama's nasty tea. She had declared you (me) too ill to do home school and banished you to bed. Poor Kat, I guess you didn't have much of a day off.

When you came home from school the following afternoon, your face was like thunder.

'What did you do to me?' you cried. 'What did you *do*?'

I stared at you. What were you talking about?

But as you told me what happened it all began to make sense.

When you got in, you sat where you always sat. In the front row.

All morning you could hear whispering behind you, you said. But when you turned to share in your friends' secret chatter, the other girls stopped talking. They looked at you with unfriendly eyes. Something was wrong.

At lunch time, you took a tray of food and went to join your friends at your usual table. But nobody had saved a chair for you. In fact, they all looked through you as if you'd become invisible.

Embarrassed, you turned away, pretending that you'd forgotten something.

And then you saw her. In the far corner of the cafeteria. Mila. She was waving and pointing at the seat she'd reserved at her table.

'Kara, you sat with *her*! You ignored *my* friends!' Kat raged. 'Mila is not my friend, Kara. She's *nothing*. I've never spoken to her. Now what am I supposed to do with a friend I don't want?'

But . . . but *I* had liked Mila. Surely you would like Mila too, if you gave her half a chance.

But you were beyond reasoning with. When my hands flew up to explain, you held both my wrists and stopped me. You didn't want to know.

'How am I going to make things go back to the way they were?' you complained. 'You've ruined everything! You've ruined my life! You were only borrowing my identity for the day. Now you've made me the laughing stock of the class and I will *never ever* swap places with you again.'

Your fingers were tight on my wrists. I struggled but, of course, I couldn't talk back. Couldn't say anything to reassure you. Not that I wanted to.

Kat, we were so alike, you and I. We liked the same colours, the same clothes; liked the same shows on TV, the same books, the same music.

You could have been me.
And that afternoon, long ago, I wished it were so.
I wished that you were the chosen one.
That the Calm had claimed you instead of me.

7

Every evening as darkness swallowed the mountain, I knelt at the windowsill to light the candles for Mother. I always pretended that my withered throat was whole, that words took shape when I whispered, that the sounds that issued from my lips were not rasping grunts but language that made perfect sense.

As I flicked the lighter and one candle after another sputtered into flame, I shivered with anticipation. I had news for Mother tonight.

Mother, I whispered. *I think I've got a friend.*

The candles were new and their waxy teardrop tips were still perfect, unmelted by the yellow flames. Their wicks caught fire quickly, and when I switched off the overhead light they glowed bright and strong in the window.

He's nice, Mother. Very good at photography. You would like him.

I cupped my hands around my eyes to shield them

from the candle glow, to speed their adjustment to the blackness outside the window. I couldn't see the ocean but I could hear it breathing quietly. The rain rustled and trees swished in the wind. There was a distant pinpoint of light on the promenade where the only working street light had switched on. Slowly, slowly, my eyes got used to the darkness. *Mother, I whispered, are you there?*

As I did every night, I waited for a shape to appear, a smiling face upturned to the candle light, a hand raised, waving.

Tonight, Mother? Will you come tonight? Please?

But in the gloom below me there was nothing.

It was Yaya who gave me the idea.

I was just five when she first came to work for us after Mother died, and at first impression she seemed so self-assured, sturdy, unafraid. A strapping old boot.

But come nightfall on Yaya's first day, to our surprise she turned into a cowering, scaredy old thing.

We were all sitting around the dining table when she suddenly jumped up with eyes round and staring like fried eggs. She rushed to the living room and began dragging curtains over the windows. As she hurried up the stairs she called over her shoulder by way of explanation, 'We don't want them looking in.'

'*Them?* Who are you talking about?' Father asked.

'Ghosts, of course!' she said, glaring at him like he'd asked a stupid question.

Father looked like he'd just swallowed a bone. But I was fascinated. Ghosts?

This was how Yaya explained them:

When the dead have unfinished business – a crime unconfessed, a message undelivered, an apology unspoken – their souls get stuck on Earth.

Ghosts hide by day and emerge at night, searching for the life force that has gone from them. That's why they follow the living around at night. And that's why they are drawn to candle flames. A candle's flicker and heat has the same throb of life.

'Why do you think we light candles in churches, eh, Rosa?' Yaya said. 'The spirits cannot help themselves, they follow the light, enter the church, and once inside the angels and saints can sort them out. Give them a leg up to Heaven.'

Whenever darkness fell in that first month that she lived with us, Yaya rushed around the house, slamming shutters and drawing the curtains. 'Don't let them see the lights!' she exclaimed. 'Have a mercy on those poor lost souls!'

She refused to go out at night. 'I can feel them behind me! I can feel a coldness hovering there, I can feel something breathing on the back of my neck.'

'Yaya!' Father protested. 'How can you believe in such claptrap?'

But that only made Yaya dig a fist into her pocket and produce a handful of salt. 'This is what you need,' she cried. 'Salt! It throws their sense of direction, halts them in their tracks!' And then she sprinkled it over her shoulder.

Father couldn't stand it. Every evening when he got home, he swept up the white trail Yaya had laid across the front doorway. 'This has got to stop, Yaya,' he barked. 'This is going to cost us a *fortune* in salt. It's a wonder the ocean's still salty at the rate you're using the stuff up.'

But without the salt Yaya became a bundle of tics and nerves, startling at the smallest noise, listening to every rustle and thud around the house.

'*Jesus Mary Joseph!*' she would yelp, crossing herself, when a sharp blast of wind through bamboo turned into an eerie moan, or if the branch of a tall acacia rapped sharply on the window pane.

And I would run to her side and slip my hand into hers.

One night when I was ten, I was startled out of bed by a series of sharp screams from Yaya's room.

I heard the clumsy stumble of Father climbing out of bed next door. I leaped to follow, and as I fumbled to open my door I could hear Father's deep voice outside, agitated at first, then soothing, as Yaya responded in high-pitched squeaks, like an unhappy mouse.

I came out into the hall to find Father gesticulating in the doorway of Yaya's room. 'Look, Yaya, look, it's just your dress on that hanger,' he said. 'You had your electric fan on too high and it blew the dress onto your bed.'

'No.' Yaya was sitting up, her sheet drawn to her chin, her yellow skin paled to the colour of coffee with too much milk in it. 'I *SAW* her. *I saw her with my own EYES!*'

My hands were signing frantically like flapping birds. *Who? Who was in the room with Yaya?*

I pushed past Father and Yaya looked at me with eyes the size of dinner plates. '*It was your DEAD MOTHER, Rosa,*' she cried. '*She was sitting at the*

FOOT OF MY BED. May the Lord have mercy on us.'

I was so amazed that I couldn't stop myself from crying out. '*Ungh ungh ungh!*' I rushed towards the bed, throwing myself on the floor to search under it, patting all the lumps to see what hid under the sheet, opening and closing the wardrobe doors.

But Father was right. Mother was nowhere to be seen.

And there was Yaya's dress with its blue and green diamond pattern, on a hanger dangling from the wardrobe handle. The electric fan had indeed blown it askew. Its long skirt draped gracefully over the end of the bed and I half expected legs to appear beneath the hem. Every time the electric fan oscillated in its direction, the dress stirred, shrugging its shoulders and rearranging its skirts.

I stared at it in dismay. So it *wasn't* Mother?

'You've frightened Rosa now. See, what did I tell you?' Father grumbled.

But Yaya already had her arms around me. 'Don't be scared, little Rosa, it's all right. Your daddy is right, there are no ghosts in this room.'

The truth was, I could barely contain myself. Yaya had given me an idea. A *wonderful* idea. It was all I could do not to laugh out loud.

All I needed was a candle to light. And a window for it to shine in. Then perhaps Mother's ghost would come to see me.

I told them my plan after breakfast the following morning when we were marching about, clearing the table.

Of course, I knew that Father would hate the idea. I was totally prepared for his snort of derision, and the superior way he said, 'BUT THERE ARE NO SUCH THINGS AS GHOSTS!'

But I had not expected opposition from Yaya. She was always looking for ghosts, wasn't she?

She was frightened last night – but only because it was so unexpected. Otherwise, she would *like* Mother, even if she was a ghost. Mother would be a good, kind spirit, I was sure of it! How many times had Yaya said, 'Oh, I wish I'd met Mam Kara before she died.' Well, this was just her wish come true.

But, no. The horror on Yaya's face was a sight to behold. She was scowling so hard her forehead knitted together like rope. Her mouth was turned down so severely I was afraid the corners would join under her chin and then her lower jaw would fall off.

'Oh *no*, Rosa,' she said in a voice so sharp with revulsion Father jumped. And then it was as if she couldn't stop the long moan that streamed from her throat. 'Nononononononononooooo.'

'Yaya!' Father admonished. 'No need to be so dramatic.'

But once she started, Yaya couldn't stop. 'This is not good! Not good, Rosa! *The dead are dead!* We have no business with them. Leave it to the churches to summon the spirits!'

She was actually shaking, her normally narrow eyes round as buttons, her skin blanched, sweat shining on her forehead. I half expected her to collapse into a steaming heap on the floor.

Father looked at her helplessly. He raised an arm as if he was going to put it round her but then seemed to change his mind. 'There there, Yaya,' he soothed finally, pulling a chair from the dining table. 'Sit here. Let me get you some tea. Try not to think about it.'

Yaya sat down, both hands clasped in front of her, rocking a little. 'Maybe she won't come? Maybe Mam Kara's spirit won't see the candles?' she muttered to herself.

It made me cross. *Mother will come*, I signed emphatically.

Father glared at me from where he was pouring out the tea. 'Well . . .' he said, carefully laying the cup in front of Yaya. 'Let's talk about this later, OK? OK, Yaya?'

She nodded and wrapped her hands around the china cup. Father patted me on the head and fled out the door with such a sigh of relief I almost burst out laughing. Even after five years of living with Yaya, Father found her outbursts mysterious and confusing.

Yaya just sighed a heavy sigh and turned to me. 'Why do you want trouble, Rosa?' she said, her voice now controlled and even. 'The dead must not be encouraged to stay on this earth. We must set them free.'

And then she told me the story of the monkey's paw.

8

'Rosa, my own sainted mother told me this story, may the Lord bless her soul. She read it in an old book that belonged to Padre Pio, the old missionary who ran the school in her village. I only tell you this from my own imperfect memory . . .'

One day a farmer came home from the market all in a fluster.

'Missis!' he called to his old wife. 'Missis, here at last is the answer to all our troubles!'

His wife emerged from their shabby little kitchen at once. 'Oh, my goodness! What is it? What have you got?'

The farmer held out something small and wizened and black.

And do you know what it was, Rosa? It was a tiny hand, black as old tar, wrinkles scored all over its leathery skin like a map, with miniature, broken, black fingernails and a thick fringe of coarse black hair ringing the wrist.

A monkey's paw.

The woman jumped backwards. It was worse than stumbling upon a dead rat in the garden. 'If you think this is funny, you foolish old man, you are mistaken!' she cried. 'Get rid of it at once!'

But the old man clutched the paw to his chest. His eyes gleamed. '*No!* I bought it from a merchant seaman at the market who swore that it had worked for him. It grants three wishes!'

The old woman groaned, silently saying a Hail Mary before asking, 'Why are you such a sucker for these things? Who do you think you are, Jack and the Beanstalk?'

(You know Jack with his Beanstalk, Rosa? The boy who exchanged his mother's cow for magic beans?)

But the old man just laughed. He held the ugly black thing up to the sky, closed his eyes and made his first wish: 'I wish we had FIVE THOUSAND PESOS!'

His wife rolled her eyes and turned away, shaking her head. 'I won't even ask you how much you paid the merchant seaman. I have better things to do. Alberto will be home soon, desperate for his lunch. At least *he* will have done a good morning's work, at the factory. Lucky he didn't take after his foolish father.'

The old man didn't reply; he just followed her to the kitchen, set the monkey's paw down on the table and sat down, his face alert, waiting.

Ten minutes passed. Fifteen minutes. Twenty. Nothing.

The old man's head sank low in his shoulders. But then, as the rusty clock on the wall ticked past the hour, there was a knock on the door. He leaped to his feet, his face expectant, heaving a sigh of relief before he opened the door.

But there was only a sweaty young man clad in the uniform of Alberto's factory. 'Sir, you are Alberto's father?'

The old man's wife hurried out of the kitchen. 'What is it? What has happened?' she cried, knowing in her mother's heart that it had to be something terrible.

'I am sorry, mam. Alberto ... Alberto fell into some cutting machinery. He was badly hurt.' The young man couldn't hold their stricken gazes. He looked away.

'Where is he? Which hospital?' the woman shouted, tearing off her apron, ready to go instantly to her son's side.

'Mam . . . he is dead, mam.'

The two old people crumpled together as if someone had suddenly chopped away their legs, the woman keening like a stray cat. Her husband could only hold her in his own shaking arms.

Tears appeared in the messenger's eyes. It was several moments before he could speak. 'Mam, sir, I am sorry. Everyone at the factory is upset. We passed a hat around. We want to give you this.' And he held out an envelope.

The old man snatched the envelope from him. But even before he'd opened it, he knew what it contained.

Five thousand pesos.

It was only in the hours after their son was buried that the old couple remembered the monkey's paw.

'This is all your fault, you old fool,' the old woman said between wracking sobs. 'What will we do with five thousand pesos now? What is the point when the most precious thing in our lives has been taken away? Throw that horrible thing into the fire – it has brought us nothing but misery.'

But an obstinate look came over the old man's face. 'I can fix this, missis. I can fix this!' He grabbed

the monkey's paw and squeezed it hard. 'I WISH
OUR SON ALIVE AGAIN!'

They stared at each other, the old man's eyes
daring his wife to resist. But instead she ran to the
door. 'Alberto! Come to us, Alberto!'

But there was nobody outside, nothing to see
except the hardening curtain of rain over the bamboo
thicket. The old man joined his wife and together
they waited at the open door.

One hour passed.

Two.

Nothing.

It wasn't going to happen. Numbly the old man
put his arm round his wife's shoulders and turned her
away from the door. He pulled it shut and drew the
bolt across the top.

The woman's head suddenly jerked up. 'What's
that?'

'What?'

'I heard something.'

They listened. And sure enough there it was. A
soft scraping. A slow shuffling footfall on the path
approaching their door.

The old woman threw her head back and laughed
an ecstatic, triumphant laugh. 'Of course! It's two

kilometres from the cemetery! It would have taken Alberto a long long time to get here.'

Crying and laughing she threw herself at the door and began to unfasten the latch.

But the old man grabbed her by the shoulders. 'No! Don't open that door, woman!'

'What do you mean? It's Alberto! Our Alberto!'

He stared at her. She could only see the bright and shining return of their dear Alberto, such a beautiful young man. But . . . but . . . he was mangled by the machinery, wasn't he? Beyond recognition. His skin flayed, his limbs twisted. It had been ten days since the accident. And the cemetery had been a mud bath in the rain. It would have taken their son's rotting, broken corpse an age to muddle its way to their house.

The old man snatched up the monkey's paw and breathed his third and last wish. And as his wife finally managed to unbolt the door, he ran to the fire in the kitchen and threw in the paw.

As he watched it catch fire, filling the kitchen with a pungent, burning stink, his wife's cries pierced the night.

'Alberto! *Alberto!* Oh, where have you gone? Where are you, Alberto?'

*   *   *

'Rosa, the dead must remain dead. Please. Let us not invite your mother back.' Yaya opened her arms wide and waited for me to give her a hug.

But I just glared at her. Good story. Spine-chilling as they came. And she told it well with the right stops and gasps and showing the whites of her eyes.

But come come, Yaya. It was a *zombie* story. Which had nothing to do with ghosts.

Yaya's idea of a ghost was one that suddenly appeared, screaming, out of the darkness.

Which was stupid, really. Mother's spirit would never *ever* say boo. I should know. All those years ago in the market, when Mother had died, she had showed herself to me. I had *seen* Mother's ghost.

And that was why I wanted to light the candles. I knew her ghost was out there. I just wanted to see her again.

9

L ove is patient. Love is kind.

Yaya read that to me a long time ago from her old Bible and it's stuck in my brain ever since like an annoying song.

Love is patient. And I *was* patient! I kept the faith, didn't I? As the years unfurled and the sun rose and fell behind Banawa and the candles burned and Mother didn't come and didn't come and didn't come.

And then after a while, Mother not coming became the default. Just part of the schedule. And the candle-lighting became a habit hard to break. Something I did at the end of a day. It marked the end of sunlight activities – chores and studies and leisure – and the beginning of evening things – dinner, time with Father, TV.

So the daily disappointment of not seeing a friendly, motherly ghost? It didn't hurt. It was just the way things were.

Father objected to the candles in the beginning, of course, but not for very long. He backed off quickly enough, like he always did. He probably decided it wouldn't do me any harm. That I would outgrow the idea eventually. Or stop believing. Whichever came first.

But Yaya took it more personally, so it took a bit more time for her to stop being so tense and snarky. As time passed, though, she became used to the candles. It became as much of a habit for her as it was for me. She rarely mentioned it, and when she did it was only to make sure I'd blown the flames out before we sat down for supper.

It suited me not to have Yaya worrying so I tried not to remind her of the candles. Best not to create upset where there wasn't any.

But it would have been useful to ask Yaya *why* Mother's spirit had not come. What was holding her up? Was she waiting for something? Or someone?

Mother, come to me, Mother!

Love is PATIENT.

So, did Ansel95 like me?

Well, would he hang around if he didn't?

After the first few times we exchanged messages, I quickly realized that friendship was, like all things, something that needed practice.

Practice makes . . . well, not perfect, but at least not incompetent.

Ansel95 of course was operating on the basis that the girl on the other side of the ether was someone well-versed in the give and take of relationships, who'd made and lost friends, who knew how to live among living, breathing creatures her own age.

Who was I to tell him otherwise?

> Hey.

That was how he always started out. He was cooler than even our American-style fridge with the freezer compartment four inches thick with ice no matter how many times Yaya and I defrosted it.

And I matched him cool for cool.

> Hey.

Of course, I wanted to say it with an exclamation point, 'Hey!' or in caps 'HEY!!!!!' because that was how I felt whenever his bubble plopped up on the screen.

But it wouldn't do, would it? Just because I'd been living in a tower all my life was no excuse for turning into a gushing, shouting, dribbling, drooling thing. Pathetic. Me.

What's up, Strop?

Nothing. What about you?

Everything. My life is a storm.

Drama queen!

She jests at scars that never felt a wound.

What scars? What wound?

> Dude, aren't you even impressed?

> Romeo and Juliet. Balcony scene. I did that in English too. And don't call me dude.

I was tempted to say the correct line was, '*He* jests at scars' not, '*She* jests at scars'. Romeo was talking about Mercutio, wasn't he? How Mercutio was making fun of him.

Was this friendship, then? Sitting and talking about nothing in particular. Laughing about random things. Passing the time?

It felt . . . great! The world seemed a little bit roomier. Like the walls of the attic had been pushed farther away. Like the view in the window had suddenly become a bit wider. Like the computer screen had doubled in size.

And time . . . well, time ticked by – even ROARED by, like those jumbo jets that were always flying over the island. One minute I was switching on the laptop, the next it was time for bed.

Yaya was right about my 388 friends being imaginary. Because Ansel95 was a whole new world. He definitely wasn't a figment. He occupied time and space. He was a gift.

> So. Who is the Ansel in Ansel95?

> How do you know my real name ISN'T Ansel?

> Of course it isn't.

> I never questioned yours. I mean . . . Stroppyweather. Common name, I know plenty of Stroppies.

> What's a few pseudonyms between friends?

Ansel Adams.

Ansel who?

I believe in beauty. I believe in stones and water, air and soil, people and their future and their fate.

Eh?

Ansel Adams said that.

He did?

Yup. The real Ansel was a photographer.

What a surprise.

Sarcasm is unattractive and I will ignore yours. His name was Ansel Adams and he was really cool. Come, let me show you.

He did something, and like magic I could see his screen. He was some kind of conjuror, reaching across the wi-fi, replacing my desktop with his.

I stared at his desktop as he set up the Ansel Adams album. It was just that one glorious photo of Banawa and nothing else. So neat. So unlike mine which was littered with tiny icons. It made me feel odd, seeing his stuff. It was like peeking into his bedroom. Like we'd touched hands by mistake. Like our eyes had met by accident. It made my heart beat faster, and for a long while I couldn't focus on the images he was showing me, couldn't read his message bubbles bouncing up on the screen.

I felt over-excited, overstimulated, overstretched. Poor hermit girl, unused to the company of others, suddenly having to cope with human company. I groaned, clutching my belly as if I'd eaten something bad. Urgh. Stop it, Rosa! Get a hold of yourself or he's going to notice. Calm down!

When I finally did manage to pay attention to the Ansel Adams photographs, I could have swooned.

He showed me photo after magnificent photo of amazing landscapes in black and white, the blacks really black and the whites glowing with some kind of inner light. There were glowering clouds curling across massive skies, long low shafts of light carving scenery into undulating shapes, and soaring mountains that stood and stared. Like Banawa.

Ansel Adams.
Remember the name.
And these were in the 1920s and 30s. He took pictures with a camera the size of his head.

Wow. Respect.

Ansel Adams made me want to take pictures.

He makes me want to take pictures too. He's great.

You know what, his mum didn't get him at all. She didn't want him to go into photography.

Really? But he's amazing.

Yeah.

We lingered over one mountain for a whole minute before another bubble appeared.

> **My mum's kind of that way too. She doesn't like me going everywhere, taking pictures. But I do it anyway.**

> **Mums are blind to talent.**

The moment I said it, I knew it was a mistake. You idiot, Rosa! You've opened a door and crooked a finger! And sure enough, Ansel95 followed me in.

> **So. Have you got a mum problem too?**

What could I possibly say? That my mother was dead? That she was a ghost? That I was trying to lure her home every evening with candles?

> **Hey, Stroppy? Are you still there?**

Oops. Dinner's on the table. Sorry, I've got to go. See you tomorrow, Ansel Boy.

And I logged off before he could follow up with another question.

10

That night, I stared at the picture of Mother in the silver frame that had sat on my bedside table since for ever.

I was five years old in the photo, smiling on Mother's lap. Identical scarves were looped round our necks. Mother had had the photo framed for Father's birthday. In the corner of the photo, she'd scribbled a dedication, her handwriting long and slanting in silver ink on the dark background: *To Jon, with all our love, K and R.*

Father popped his head in. 'Night-night, Rosa.'

I waved.

'You want me to switch off your overhead light?'

I nodded and he flicked the switch by the door. The room immediately plunged into cool blue darkness, my room suddenly the deepest part of the ocean and the frame on the table a glint of treasure.

I continued to stare, even though I couldn't see Mother any more. Somehow the darkness seemed to be filled with far more truth than the light. I sighed. Every year that passed, every minute that ticked by, it got harder and harder to remember Mother. The memory of her had turned into something faded in the back of my head. It scared me.

If I didn't deliberately reach in, pull the memories out to examine now and then, I knew that Mother would simply fade away to nothing.

You have to come back, Mother! Please come back! If you don't come . . . I pushed my face into the pillow. All I would have left would be *that* night.

Instead of all the other happy thoughts I could have about Mother, my mind always conjured up the one memory I could definitely live without, rushing with blood and fear and sorrow. No, no, no. Not again.

I grabbed the picture frame and hugged it to my chest, trying to think of something, ANYTHING else. But the memory simply stretched, sat down, crossed its legs. Made itself more comfortable for the telling.

It was an unusually bright day. I remember how the rain cast a strange dapple of shadows on the walls of the attic.

I was five and the attic room was still done up like

a living room. My bookcases, desk and computer – these were still long in the future. Instead, there was a sofa, my baby drawings taped up on the wall, and my toys scattered all over the floor.

It was lunch time and Mother decided we were going to have a picnic right there on the attic floor. I remember helping her spread the rug, laying out plates of sandwiches cut into triangles, slices of sweet yellow mango, cartons of juice, crackers. There was coffee in a flask for Mother and warm creamy chocolate for me in a beaker.

We'd only just arranged ourselves, cross-legged on the rug, when suddenly everything around us changed colour.

Everything turned a shade of gold. I remember the walls, the ceiling, the window frame – how they glowed. It made me gasp with wonder. And then I became a little bit worried. I'd never seen anything like it.

Mother leaped to her feet and stood there by the window for a long moment, her face pressed against the casement glass, staring up at the sky.

I clambered to her side and tugged at her blouse. *What?* I signed. Mother smiled down at me and signed. *Look, look!*

She pushed the windows open, then picked me up to show me.

The clouds were changing from their usual shades of grey to a bright white, as if something beyond was rinsing out all the dirt.

And there it was. The sun, edging out slyly from between two clouds.

It was white with heat, shining fiercely through the thin screen of rain, a silver disc expanding. And as it grew the clouds around it melted away to nothing, taking the rain with them, revealing a blue sky.

At first there was a *drip drip* noise everywhere. And then even the dripping sound ceased. The rain had stopped.

I remember every detail. The dryness of the heat, the glare of so much light, the spangle of so many reflections on the sea, the way the mountain turned a pastel shade of green; the way the shadows leached away to nothing, the mountain face erased by the flat brightness above.

Suddenly Mother was bustling around the room. I watched with goldfish eyes, wondering what she was up to.

She snatched up her pink flowered scarf and

arranged it artfully over the marks of the Calm on her neck.

She pulled me onto her lap, tied my hair back, exactly like hers. Then she produced another scarf, pink and flowered just like hers, and arranged it round my neck.

She carried me to the mirror and pressed her cheek against mine, giggling.

We looked so alike! Big Mother and little Mother. I laughed out loud.

Mother lifted me up on her hip and carried me downstairs where she put a hand on the front door latch.

I stared at her, wide-eyed.

But we were not allowed! Not at this time of the day . . . and not without Father. Didn't Father say it wasn't safe? Didn't we always wait until he got home from work before we dared go out on the deserted beach?

But Mother's fingers were working fast. She unbolted the long barrel, lifted the latch, pushed the door open, took my hand and . . .

Suddenly we were standing outside on the pavement. *Outside*.

I found myself gasping. I'd been holding my breath

without realizing it. I clung to Mother's hand so hard that she bent down to kiss my little fist, stroking it until I loosened my grip.

I remember the smell of earth drying, the warmth of steam rising from the road. I remember the empty sky which looked strange without its canopy of restless grey cloud.

The absence of the rain's monotone made every other sound sharp and crisp.

The world was suddenly echoing with a thousand separate noises. I could hear every clunk and click and twitter, every hiss of breath, every doggy whimper, every scrape of a chair leg.

And how the sun shone, hard and white in a flat blue sky.

Mother tugged on my hand and we began to walk.

She took me down the path to the promenade and the beach. The midday heat pressed against my skin. I made faces, puffing out my cheeks and working my lips against its warm weight. It was strange. It was delicious.

The beach lay broad and white beyond the promenade, the sea swishing invitingly in the distance. I looked up at Mother and she nodded, laughing.

We raced out onto the beach, leaping and twirling

on the soft sand. We took off our sandals and chased each other where soft waves licked at the beach, smoothing it down. The wet sand sucked at our toes and we laughed some more.

So much space, so much *air*! I raced ahead of Mother, head thrown back, feeling the breeze in my hair. I could have run and run and never stopped.

Mother followed, swinging our sandals in one hand as I skipped in and out of the waves, exclaiming at every splash, stopping to examine every pebble, every squiggle of seaweed, every clamshell in the sand.

I held my arms out at the sun, the better to feel the heat. But then the heat began to prickle, and then to burn. I found myself trying to shield my arms from the sun with fingers spread wide like fans.

Mother took my hand and hurried us into the shade of nearby coconut trees.

And there in the cooling shadows, I had my next big surprise of the day.

People.

So many of them, walking and talking under blue tarpaulins tied to the swaying coconut trunks.

There were rows of tented stalls beneath the ranks

of trees, with ropes of onions, garlic and other tantalizing stuff strung above baskets and tables laden with colourful goods.

So many things! So many people!

I felt like I was suddenly surrounded by an army of soldier ants. I huddled behind Mother's skirts.

But Mother gently urged me forward, taking my hand.

We walked slowly past the stalls, watching the people surreptitiously, and admiring the things that peeked like promises from the baskets, marvelling at the colours of everything.

We were standing next to a stall hung with splendid bouquets of chilli peppers when Mother's head suddenly snapped up.

I whirled round, trying to see what she had seen.

She straightened up, a flush suddenly blooming under the brown skin. She put her hands on my shoulders and stood me next to a basket of woven hats. Her eyes were glowing, excited.

Wait here, she signalled. *Back soon.* She flashed me a big smile and waved as she hurried out of sight behind another stall.

I waited, quite happy to stare at the hats in the basket, thinking about the beach and the waves and all the things we had just seen and done in the sunshine.

The minutes ticked past.

And then it was as if time began to sag. My neck itched and I fingered the scarf round my neck. The sea breeze didn't blow here under the tarpaulins. It was too hot.

Worry began to gnaw.

Where was Mother?

Looking up, I could only see the flapping green of the tarpaulins, the faces of strangers, the blue of the sky in the gaps between the stalls.

And then I noticed the khaki uniform beside me. A policeman fingering the leather straps of his holster. He seemed anxious, full of dread, staring at the blue sky, shaking his head, frowning.

He caught sight of me and smiled. 'Are you lost, little one?' His brown face was kindly under the peak of his hat.

'Are you lost?'

I continued to look around for Mother, panic now fluttering like a trapped sparrow in my chest.

The policeman bent down so that his face was level with mine. 'Are you looking for your mama?'

I nodded.

'There's a police station just around the corner. That's where your mama will go looking for you. Shall I take you there?'

My fear dissipated. He was right. Mother would be looking for me, frantic with worry. He could help me.

But as I reached to take the policeman's outstretched hand, the scarf Mother had so carefully arranged round my neck slipped down.

And he saw.

'Oh my God.' He breathed out the words, his face grey. He snatched his hand away and his other hand suddenly clamped onto the pistol holstered at his hip.

I didn't hesitate. That look on his face. The sudden electricity that jangled between us. His terror. I recognized the danger immediately. In that moment I understood with a fearful clarity why Mother and I never stepped out of the house.

I ran.

I could remember every line on the policeman's brown face, the way he was suddenly grinding his teeth, the way his eyebrows disappeared into his hat as his eyes grew wide with horror.

As I ran, I waited to hear the bang from his pistol, waited to feel the thud of a bullet in my back.

And behind me the shouts multiplied and soon I could hear the baying of excited dogs.

I heard the shouting in the distance, felt the trickle of sweat down my back, my heart pounding in my chest, every intake of breath scalding my lungs as I ran for my life.

And then my legs buckled under me, unable to carry me any further. With one last burst of energy, I threw myself behind a tall basket, crouching low, my fists against my mouth to silence my sobbing.

There was a touch on my shoulder and I stifled a scream.

But the woman peering down at me only gestured. 'Quick, little one, this way,' she mumbled. She wore a shawl that covered her mouth, muffling her voice.

I tried to stand but my legs folded under me like broken straws. I was so tired that my breaths were coming in little gasps.

The woman reached down to pick me up, and as she wrapped her arms around me in a tight hug, the shawl over her mouth dropped.

I stared.

Her top lip was split, like someone had taken a pair of scissors and snipped it to reveal the teeth below.

'It's OK,' she whispered, and there was something

in her tone that made me believe her. Everything was going to be OK. She lifted me up and I clung to her, thinking of Mother.

'Shh, it's all right.' She stroked my back and jiggled me a little like a baby she was putting to sleep. 'Don't cry, sweetheart. Everything is going to be all right.'

She carried me behind her stall, which was packed with baskets of every description. Looking quickly over her shoulder, she lifted me up and into a tall narrow basket with a domed lid on a hinge. I huddled down deep in the hot, airless wicker.

'Sit quietly.' She put her finger to her lips. 'Not a sound now.'

I nodded, putting my thumb in my mouth so that it wouldn't make a noise.

She fitted the lid over me. The sudden darkness was comforting, with only thin milky strips of light seeping through the weave. I could just about see through to the world outside. *Mother, where are you?*

The thunder of running feet came closer. The men breathed noisily, like the herds of horses on a nature programme I once saw. They were so close I could smell the odour of their sweat as they ran past the entrance of the stall.

Khaki legs entered. 'Did you see her?' It was the policeman who had wanted to help me until my scarf had slipped. Only this time his voice had lost the soft edge of kindness. 'A child. With the marks of the Calm on her neck.'

I could not see the woman, but her voice was muffled so I knew she was keeping her split lip covered. 'Oh, no! Oh, my goodness, is that what you are all running around for?'

'Did you see her?'

'No. I didn't see her.'

The khaki legs scissored away quickly and I heard him shouting to the others. 'You! Check behind those stalls. You! Try that side of the market. We mustn't let her get away.'

I wondered that he could not hear the loud knocking of my heart.

Then the khaki legs returned. They were so close I could have poked a finger out of the basket and touched his knee.

'Sister, may I trouble you for a glass of water?'

'Of course you may, officer.'

And I listened as the woman oh so slowly poured water into a glass.

'I thought she was a lost child. I was about to take

her to the station.' I could hear his thirsty gulps, his lips smacking. 'Luckily I saw the marks on her neck. God saved me.' His hands made the sign of the cross across his chest. Then there were more water sounds. When he finished, he sighed a long sigh. 'You know the stories. If the rains stop, look out, demons become bolder.'

'And what are you going to do with her when you catch her?' The woman's voice was casual, as if she was discussing the price of rice.

The man did not answer. I could hear gulps as he drank more water.

She tried again. 'What will you do to the child?'

'It's not a child, miss. It's a *thing*. Dangerous. They can take all shapes.'

'So what will you do with . . . *it?*'

The policeman's voice, when he finally answered, sounded slightly offended. Like the answer was too obvious.

'What would *you* do if you caught a monster?'

11

What would you do if you caught a monster?

The words echoed in my ears as I crouched in that basket watching fearfully through the slats of the wicker.

I slept a bit and in my dreams, the terror continued. I was awakened by the basket's lid being swept aside and the bright light of a single kerosene lamp in the darkness.

'Come on out, sweetheart.' It was my rescuer, stroking my hair with her fingers.

But I couldn't move. My soft five-year-old bones felt like they had hardened to brittle sticks. How long had I been hiding? It could have been minutes and it could have been hours.

She lifted me out gently and I whimpered.

The woman held me close, her cheek against mine. Her scarf dropped away, baring her disfigured lips, but I didn't care, cuddling up to the comfort of her, the kindness.

Night wrapped the market now, with only the occasional snuffle of faraway animals and the strident roar of the occasional motorbike.

A tarpaulin fell over half of the doorway. There was a street light outside, and over the woman's shoulder I could see that rain had begun to fall.

Something moved in the shadows outside and I jumped out of her arms, edging up to the doorway, ready to run again.

'Shh,' the woman called behind me. 'Everybody's gone. There's hardly anyone here.'

But the thing in the shadows outside continued to advance. Suddenly I was aware of a heat in my face, in the palms of my hands and in the base of my spine. No, not heat because an icy coldness was welling around me. Electricity. It spread all over me like a thousand swarming insects making me squirm.

The shape resolved into a human shape and I held my breath.

The figure stepped into the yellow light pooling under the street lamp.

It was Mother.

To this day I remember that moment. It's as if everything slowed down, down, down. Mother, Mother, Mother, my mind murmured. She stumbled a little, rubbing a hand over her eyes. Her hair fell in an untidy sheet about her face. She looked tired and confused.

Mother, Mother, Mother.

I remember the relief that surged through me, I can still feel the lifting of that terrible cloud of fear, of anxiety, of hopelessness. I should have cried out. Run to her. But I didn't move, did I? Instead, I watched, transfixed.

She didn't stop. Kept walking.

And then I did cry out. Tore myself from the doorway. Ran outside.

But Mother had disappeared. I hurried up the path and peered down an alley between two stalls.

Where had she gone?

How had the market which was teeming with people just an hour before become so empty? Only shadows moved in its labyrinth.

I blinked, suddenly unsure about what I'd seen.

At that moment the wet air hardened and suddenly great sheets of rain came crashing down, slicing through the gaps and causing the tarpaulins to flap against the bending trunks of the coconut trees.

The woman rushed out and took my hand. 'Quick, little one, come back in here. Look, I got you some food and water while you were asleep.'

I followed her back into the stall, the mention of food awakening parts of me I'd forgotten about. I'd had nothing to eat or drink for hours. My tummy growled like a desperate little beast, and when the woman produced a bottle of water I grabbed it and drank greedily.

Then she handed me a plastic fork and a polystyrene carton full of noodles. I was so hungry I dropped the fork on the ground and ate with my fingers.

'I went to buy this while you were asleep. I was afraid you might wake up while I was gone and wander off! I was so relieved to see you were still here. It's not safe for you out there, little one,' she said. 'Eat, eat! I will keep watch.'

My saviour left me to eat and stood by the doorway, staring into the darkness. Listening.

'Child, *child!*'

She was suddenly snatching the box of noodles from me, sweeping me up into her arms. The bottle crashed to the floor, water spilling everywhere. '*Someone's coming,*' she hissed. '*Hurry! Into the basket!*'

But panic made my legs flail and the tall basket tipped over and the woman fell on her knees trying to right it and I got in the way and then it was too late because there was someone standing in the doorway, staring at us.

She put me down and pushed her body in front of me like a shield.

'Rosa?'

It was Father. A long shadow fell over his face. As he entered, it slid slowly over him like a dark veil until at last I could see his haunted blue eyes. They were wet with relief.

I threw myself across the floor into his arms.

'Oh, Rosa.' He buried a stubbled chin in my neck and I felt the prickle of his tears as he held me tight.

I craned over his shoulder, expecting Mother to follow close behind. Where was she?

Father bowed his head. He tried to put his arms round me. But his silence frightened me. Something was wrong.

I struggled to look into his face but he turned it away like he wanted to hide something. When he finally looked down at me, his blue eyes were deep and dark, like bottomless, drowning wells.

'Rosa, I don't know how to tell you this.' He took a deep breath. 'Kara . . . your mother . . . she's had an accident.'

Accident? The word made my tummy coil into itself.

Father's face was pale in the dim light. He got to his feet, his face slipping back into the shadows. 'She was hit by a car this afternoon. It was bad, Rosa. Very bad.'

I felt the woman's touch on my shoulder and somehow my hand crept into hers.

'They brought her into the hospital. They fetched me from my clinic and took me to Emergency but by the time I got there, she was . . .' His face crumpled, and he turned his face so that a long, black shadow cut across his face. 'She only just managed to tell me that you were here in the market before she . . .'

Even now, nine years later, I can still remember the soft patting noises the rain made on the tarpaulin above our heads, the spreading gloom inside the market stall.

'She died, Rosa.'

Died?

I frowned.

Mother died?

How could that be? I just saw her! Felt her! Didn't she just walk past?

Father reached for me. 'I ... I was so afraid something had happened to you too!'

But I pulled away, throwing my arms round the woman who had rescued me. I buried my wet face in her neck. The woman – and yes, it was Yaya – held me for a long, long time as the weather outside thickened.

Father stood and watched, hunched and suddenly old.

I felt sorry for him.

But the thought that kept whirling around in my head was this: Was he lying about Mother? I *saw* her. How could she be dead?

12

There was no wake, no funeral service.

A few days after that terrible night, Father carefully wrapped my neck in a scarf and put me in the car.

We drove into town. He parked in front of a building, rolled up all the windows and made me promise to keep the doors locked while he went inside.

When he came out minutes later he had a small box in his hands.

It was filled with cinders. All that was left of Mother.

'Do you want to hold it, Rosa?'

I didn't say anything but he carefully put it on my lap.

It was heavy. Once, in the garden, I'd tried picking up a brick. It was so heavy that I dropped it on my foot, and afterwards I sat on Mother's lap crying for hours.

That was what this felt like. Like a heavy brick. How could it be so heavy if Mother was all burned up?

I turned to Father. *That night*, I signed. *I saw Mother's ghost.*

Father bowed his head. He didn't look at me when he replied, 'Yes, so you told me. It was dark, Rosa. That wasn't Mother. She was in hospital by that time.'

I shook my head and my hands slammed the air emphatically. *I SAW MOTHER.*

'Yes, well,' Father muttered.

I folded my arms across my chest and Father took the box of ashes off my lap and put it in the boot of the car.

Father told me that Mother had always wanted her ashes scattered in the ocean.

She loved the thought of her soul joining the sea, he said, eyes down on the floor. 'She was romantic about it. And the way she described it, it sounded amazing.'

And then he described it the way Mother had. In sign language. His hands floating and stirring the air, painting a picture of the endlessly moving sea, the creatures living in it and Mother's soul with them, never to be lonely ever again.

So he hired a boat and we rowed out, out, out into that wide sea to tip Mother into the waves.

It was one of those days when the ocean frothed like a cauldron. Father's boat bobbed high and low. The waves raced away from the beach, away towards a horizon that stretched to everywhere. Everywhere but here.

And I hated it. I hated the thought of Mother in that sea.

How could it be? How could Mother, laughing-and-twirling-in-the-sand Mother, disappear just like that? How could Mother be replaced by a box of soot?

Father bowed his head for a long time, staring at the water. When he looked at me, there was a thin smile on his face and his eyes were red. 'She's in Heaven now,' he said.

I nodded. But inside my emotions were up in arms. Heaven? What was Heaven? Which way to Heaven? Was there a door? Where was the key? And how did anyone know it was there?

Besides, I *saw* her ghost, didn't I? Saw her in the doorway of the stall at the very time that Father said she'd already been lying in a hospital emergency room for an hour, stone-cold dead.

Father was so wrong. Mother was anywhere but in Heaven.

Father persuaded Yaya to leave her job in the market and to come live with us as our housekeeper and my nanny.

'I have no family,' she told me on her first day. 'No mother, no father. You are my family now, little Rosa.'

In a funny way Yaya knew what it was like. She too was a sort of monster in Mirasol. She was used to people pointing and laughing at her hairlip. Or shuddering and turning away, repulsed.

In fact, Father arranged to have Yaya's cleft palate operated on. When the bandage came off, she looked like someone else, someone with a permanent twisty smile, a crooked scar above her top lip. She looked so odd it was a long time before I could bear to meet her eyes.

So it was Yaya who made sure all the doors were double-locked, who was there when Father worked late into the night at the hospital, who sat me down for home school every day – taught me how to write my name, how to read, how to do sums – who made sure I never missed a dose and who recorded every milligram of medicine I'd taken.

Father was there, of course, and he took charge of all the school maths and sciences when he had the time. But he was a busy doctor – Mother was right about one thing: Father was in huge demand.

Does that mean there are hundreds of other people like me on the island? I asked him once.

He answered softly. 'The Calm is rare. It's not that there are many people here with the disease, it's just that I'm the only specialist on the island!' Which didn't answer my question.

Yaya always said it might have been better if Father had not found her. Because if she hadn't come to look after me, he might have moved back to London long ago. 'Mirasol is no place to bring up a child with the Calm,' she said to him. 'Pah! It's not like you don't have a choice. You can move to London anytime and give Rosa a normal life.'

'Choice!' Father always replied. 'That's the key word, Yaya. We *choose* to live here. What would happen to all my patients?'

To which Yaya always replied, folding her arms across her thin chest and staring at him like he had grown horns on his head: 'Yes, but what about Rosa? Who is going to save *her*?'

I'm afraid Father's patients were the least of my concerns. And a normal life? This was the only life I'd known.

What concerned me was that Mirasol was where Mother was. If we left Mirasol it would mean leaving Mother behind. And I desperately didn't want that.

13

Listen, Kat, I always knew it wasn't fair.

Mama and Papa, they loved you just as much as they loved me. We were equally loved, yes, we both knew that.

But you didn't NEED them as much as I did. In their eyes, you had the whole world. You had school and friends, and then after high school you had nursing college. And boys ringing you up and all those countries you could apply to after graduation. You had a FUTURE, Kat.

So, Mama and Papa, they felt they had to give me a little bit more, you know?

They thought they had to spend more time with me, bring me little gifts to make up for my lousy hidden-away life . . . all those little private parties we had when Mama wore her best dress and Papa served pineapple juice in wine goblets, just for fun – just for me!

And all those movie nights when we turned off all the lights and watched my favourite videos and ate buckets of popcorn. And didn't we dance until late to the stereo? Papa and Mama in each other's arms, and you and me trying out all the latest moves!

You smiled and laughed and joined in. But I could see, Kat. I could feel the sharp little teeth, the nibble of jealousy under everything. I sensed all your sideways glances.

And I was glad.

I mean, if you were me, wouldn't you want a little something extra, a little something over your perfectly-formed twin sister who was on her way to a perfectly-formed life while you were destined for . . . well, more of the same. ALWAYS more of the same the same the same.

Though, of course, for as long as Mama and Papa were there, I didn't mind. More of the same was all right.

Until the typhoon.

We were twenty-one that year. Officially adults. You were having your nice life in nursing college. And I was at home, still Mama and Papa's darling girl.

The storm hit Mirasol in the late afternoon. And it didn't sweep in and out in a few hours like the other storms. It made landfall and stayed and stayed and stayed, cutting up the island like a whirling blade, churning up the ocean, spraying dirty rain over everything, and turning the roads into torrents.

Afterwards, you asked me, 'But what were they doing out in that weather? Both of them in that stupid car?'

The way you looked at me I knew what was on your mind.

Why else would Mama and Papa rush out in bad weather than to fetch something for their favourite daughter?

We had been running low on my medication. Papa said he would do it and Mama said, like she always did, *You shouldn't be out there all by yourself, I'll go with you. The girls will be fine.*

It wasn't me who sent them out there, Kat, understand? I didn't ask them to go. I didn't make them get into the car.

The car was ancient, held together by Father's ingenuity and bits and pieces from the scrapyard. It didn't stand a chance against the gale on the winding mountain road. The police told you they managed to drive for a few miles, the typhoon pushing the car around. But then, as if bored with that entertainment, the winds flicked it off the road with monster fingers. Into a deep ravine.

There they were. And then they weren't.

You had to do everything, of course. The police. The morgue. The funeral. The paperwork. While you sorted it all out, I sat in the house behind a curtained window, my head in my hands.

Mama and Papa looked after me well in their will. Left me a modest trust fund. How they must have saved and scraped and planned just in case something was to happen to them. To make sure that even without them I would still have a good life.

They left you enough to complete your training. But that was it. Even then they were sure you could stand on your own two feet. That you didn't need them as much as I did.

But that didn't mean they loved you less, Kat, you know that, don't you?

We were both so bereft after that. So lost. And maybe I clung to you too hard, Kat. Maybe I was too needy. Maybe I held onto you too tightly. You must understand, you were my best friend . . . my ONLY friend. You were all I had.

You *must* understand.

I was lonely, without Mama and Papa. I had no one at home with me. And there you were, with all your friends. All those nights out.

So maybe I was demanding. Maybe it was unreasonable for me to think you should come home early, night after night. Maybe it was unfair for me to press you, every morning, to get home in time for dinner.

I couldn't help it, Kat. Mama and Papa had been the centre of my life and suddenly I had nothing but you.

But the more I clung to you, the more you moved away. You stayed out later and later, you became distant, preoccupied.

How was it possible for two people to be so close, to live under the same roof, and yet be so lonely?

It was desperate.

And you didn't tell me, all that time, what you were planning. You didn't tell me that you were sending out all those applications. That you were going to make that long-ago dream, to work in another country, come true. Except, now, your dream didn't include me. Now, you wanted to get away from your needy, clinging, annoying sister.

And when you got an offer from a famous hospital in London, you didn't hesitate. You leaped at it.

'What would YOU do, Kara?' you asked me that night in the kitchen, unable to stop your toe tapping impatiently on the floor as I sat sobbing. 'It's my dream job. I can't give up this chance.'

But we're twins! I signed. *You can't leave me!*

And you smirked. 'This once I've got to think of me. I have to do this for me.'

And before you got into the taxi for the airport, you made a little speech. You said all the right things about following your dream and making the best of an opportunity and how you would write me every week and phone me as much as you could. And I nodded and said I wanted the best for you too and good luck and have fun.

But I knew why you really left.

You were fed up with being half of a whole. You wanted to become your own person. You wanted to be free. Of me.

14

Ansel95 didn't mention mothers again which was a relief in a way. We could get on furiously discussing random, inconsequential things. Or poring over Ansel Adams like photo-obsessives. Well, Ansel95 was a photo-obsessive. I just followed his example like an imagination-free acolyte.

And we could have gone on this way for ever.

So maybe I got bored with the way things were. Because what happened next was all my doing.

> **Ansel Adams is awesome.**

I'd said it before but Ansel95 didn't seem to mind. His response was patient and predictable.

> **He really is.**

> **But now we've got a big problem.**

> Yeh?

> **What am I gonna call you? Now that I know about Ansel Adams I can't think of you as Ansel95 any more.**

See that? See?

It wasn't him that asked. It was me. I started it. It was me that wanted to know. I didn't have to, but I did. Knowing full well what it would lead to.

> OK.

> **OK? Waddaya mean – OK?**

> **I mean OK, Stroppy, I'm gonna tell you mine if you tell me yours.**

Why did I do that? Whatever happened to: be careful, stay safe, don't get involved?

My fingers hovered over the keyboard. Just say, forget it. Just say, I didn't mean to ask. Yaya's voice joined in like an echo. *STRANGER DANGER!*

The laptop beeped.

> **Come on, dude. No secrets between friends.**

Friends! See, you are friends, Rosa! If you can't tell the difference between this and your 388 meaningless friends online, then you might as well turn off the broadband just like Yaya always nags you to.

I sighed. I had to buy time.

> Stop calling me dude.

> At least you admit to not being a dude.

I laughed. Hah! He was just like me, collecting the clues to my identity. He was probably hoping my chest was as gravity-defying as my avatar's!

> OK. This is it, Stroppy. I'm saying it.

> Wait!

> No time like the present!

> Stop!

I suppose I could have turned the computer off, pulled the plug. But even as I protested, I held my breath, leaned forward in anticipation, staring hungrily at the screen, my heart suddenly thundering in my chest . . .

> **My name is Danny.**

I fell back in my chair.
Danny.
His name was Danny.
My friend.
Danny.
And then I watched helplessly as my fingers flew over the keyboard.

> **My name is Rosa.**

15

W hat's in a name?

A name is honesty. It's trust. It's knowing each other properly. It's knowing each other for ever.

Danny. Danny. Danny.

After we signed off, I hurried downstairs.

I suddenly needed to be with real flesh and blood people. I suddenly wanted to stand shoulder to shoulder with Yaya as we peeled potatoes by the sink, feel the warmth of her arm against mine, see the way her eyes lit up every time she glanced sideways at me.

I wanted to cuddle up against Father on the sofa, have him throw his arm absently over my shoulder as he clicked the remote, searching for something we could watch together on TV.

The world was smiling and I wanted more of it.

But as I got to the bottom of the stairs, I heard voices from behind the study's closed door. Sharp, quarrelsome. My high spirits sank like a stone. Father and Yaya were arguing again.

Father's voice rose above Yaya's. Interrupting. Belligerent. '. . . Look, it's all she's got, how can I make her turn it off?'

They were arguing about their favourite topic. Me. It wasn't just me who needed to get a life.

Yaya's voice shrilled like a bird's unpleasant squawk. 'It's *unhealthy*. All she does is sit in front of that laptop! If you let it go on, her brain will shrink to the size of a *peanut*!'

'Dammit, Yaya! I—'

I couldn't bear it. I threw open the study door.

Father looked up, shamefaced. But Yaya's expression was defiant. She didn't care that I'd heard, she'd nagged me often enough.

'Rosa!' He turned on his most soothing voice. 'We . . . we were just talking. Yaya's a bit concerned about the amount of time you spend on your laptop.'

Yaya raised an eyebrow. 'Concerned? Look at her! Her eyes are square-shaped!'

Father waved a hand at Yaya as if she was a pesky fly. 'Rosa. Darling. It's all about striking a balance, isn't it? Maybe you ought to spend some time doing other things? Reading? Listening to music? You haven't even been on the stationary bike for ages, and you need to take some exercise.'

I stared as he blathered on about all the other things I could do instead of having a social life. How was it better to cycle to nowhere instead of making friends? Father couldn't care less. He was just saying all these things to get Yaya off his back. Let them figure it out.

I turned away, shrugging.

'Rosa!' Father cried.

Yaya made a squeaky little sound in her throat like a rubber toy that had been stepped on.

I shut the door and immediately Father and Yaya began talking at the same time. I leaned against the wall and sighed. I should have stayed upstairs. If I had, I would still be enjoying my good mood.

There was a transom made of frosted glass above the front door. It cast a little rectangle of light, soft and pale like a smear of paint, on the clay-tiled floor in front of me. An invitation. Step forward, Rosa. Go on. Open it.

I stared glumly at the door. Nobody ever rang that doorbell. Father routed the outside world through his clinic at the hospital. So our front door saw no traffic. No mail. No visitors. And Yaya didn't really do friends. She went to church on Sundays and that was it. So all this talk about imaginary friends was rich coming from her.

Come to think of it, I didn't even know if we had a doorbell. How insane was that?

Hey, Danny, why don't you come on over? Maybe we could go down to the beach.

Danny would ring the doorbell (or knock if it turns out we never had one). And I would blithely open the door, maybe throw a mock curtsey, and Danny would stare at me in pretend disappointment. 'Hey, I thought you had wings!' And we would laugh our heads off.

But there would be loads of explaining to do, wouldn't there? How was I going to tell him that I had the Calm? There was no hiding *that*. And what if Danny *wasn't* as cool as he sounded? What if it was freak-at-first-sight?

But we'd spent enough time talking – I knew that I liked him. A lot. Even if he turned out to have four eyes and a horn on his forehead, I *liked* him. We would still be friends, wouldn't we?

The square of light on the tiles edged slightly closer, dimming a little. Night was closing. For the first time, I became aware of the insistent spatter of rain on the pavement outside.

And in the midst of the spattering: a scraping, shuffling noise.

I stiffened.

Scrape. Scrape.

Feet. On our front step. There was someone outside.

I took a step forward, staring at the door's latch.

Then suddenly, loudly: *DING DONG*.

Oh my God, we *did* have a doorbell.

Yaya burst out of the study even as I lunged towards the door.

'Rosa! Don't!'

But I was already struggling with the latch. In a minute, I'd unbolted the door, yanked it open.

A gust of rain blew into the hall, the cloud of wet needles stinging my eyes. The streetlight outside turned the rain into long white gashes.

The street was empty. There was nobody there.

'Jesus Mary Joseph!' Yaya grabbed me by the arm and yanked me away from the doorway. 'See, Doc? See what I say? She doesn't think!'

But Father wasn't listening. He was standing stock-still behind us, his face so white he glowed.

'Doc?' Yaya stared at him.

Suddenly Father was outside the door. He was

instantly drenched by the rain, his hair plastered flat and shining on his head and his clothes slopping about him. But he didn't seem to notice, his head whipping right and left as he searched the street.

'Is it you?' he cried in a strange, choked voice. He bolted down the road towards the three houses huddled near the corner, as if he'd seen something. 'Is it you?' he cried again.

Is it *who*?

Yaya hurried to the doorway. I followed close behind, but she was so concerned with Father she didn't swat me away. 'Doc?' she called in a scared voice.

Father was circling the street like a mad man, crossing from one pavement to the other, looking over the garden walls of the other three houses.

'Doc!' Yaya's voice was swallowed by the rushing of the rain.

Father stopped halfway down. Stood still, shoulders hunched, staring down the deserted road, yellow circles of lamp light pooling on the black asphalt.

He whirled round. It was too dark to see his face, but as he approached I could see the outline of his head and shoulders changing shape. I knew Father. He would be mortified by that show of scarediness.

By the time he got to us, he'd manage to install a small swagger in his stride.

'Sorry about that,' he said with a little smile. 'Thought it was a prankster. I hate that sort of thing.'

A prankster? In the rain? In all the years we'd lived on that lonely road, we'd never had a prankster. And hadn't Father shouted, 'Is it you?' into the night? Who was 'you'? Did he think we were totally blind? We could see that he was terrified. I steeled myself for Yaya's withering response.

But Yaya did nothing of the sort, even though she'd blanched to a pale shade of yellow. She slammed the door behind Father so hard that a tiny piece of plaster fell from the ceiling.

'Pneumonia!' she cried. 'Bronchitis! You'd better get into dry clothes, Doc, or disease will get you!'

Father didn't argue. He just did what he was told.

Which was an even stranger end to a strange episode.

16

It was Danny. I was sure of it.

He knew where I lived.

He was trying to flush me out. He was still trying to make me admit I lived on the island. But now *this*! It confirmed all my suspicions.

He must have raced to our house to ring the doorbell. I pressed my lips together. I wanted to laugh out loud. Danny *definitely* didn't live far away.

Dinner was silent.

Father barely ate, staring into space. I watched him, wondering. I'd always thought of Father as someone unflappable, someone who could deal with any problem. But to look at him now . . . he looked like a lost boy. I felt so sorry for him, and a little bit guilty; he looked like one of those trapped souls in a zombie apocalypse movie.

Several times, I was tempted to 'fess up about Danny. But I managed to stop myself. Father would be furious that I'd been live chatting with a stranger. He was perfectly capable of confiscating my laptop for the duration of my childhood.

Yaya, on the other hand, couldn't seem to stop talking. It was as if someone had flicked a switch on the back of her head that made words flow out of her nonstop. Like diarrhoea.

See that see that. We cannot know what is out there in the dark. The spirits oh the spirits they are waiting for their chance. You must never open the door again Rosa let me do it or let Doc do it but not you not you not you.

After long minutes of Yaya monologuing, I was just as zoned out as Father and only just registered that dinner had come to an end because Yaya had whipped my plate away.

After dinner, Father followed me to the bedroom. 'You're not to worry about this, Rosa,' he said. I began to sign, trying to say that I wasn't worried at all, but he was so busy being anxious he didn't notice.

'It's going to be OK,' he said. 'It's probably a short in the bell's wiring. I will have a look and get it fixed tomorrow when I get back from work.'

And then he gave me a big, tight hug.

After what seemed like a moment too long, he

withdrew, his hands on my shoulders, his eyes fixed on mine. 'Everything will be *FINE*.'

I watched, open-mouthed, as he brushed a tear from his eye before turning to go downstairs.

I bit my lip. Danny had no idea what a to-do he'd caused with his prank. I couldn't wait to tell him.

In the morning, I came down to breakfast to find a thick cordon of salt in the doorway and along the bottom of the stairs. Yaya was in Ghostbusters over-drive.

I'd barely sat down at the table when she thrust a handful of salt at me. 'Here, keep this in your pocket *at all times*.' And she stood there waiting until I'd shoved the stuff into my jeans pocket.

Before Father left for work, he turned to Yaya: 'Make sure the front door is locked.'

'Of course it's locked!' Yaya replied.

Father's eyes turned into hard, blue stones. He spoke through stiff lips. 'Please. Yaya. Will you. Check it. Make sure it's *locked*.' And then he stomped out the door.

Yaya and I looked at each other as the roar of Father's old station wagon faded down the road. It wasn't like him to be testy about door locking. Being neurotic about security was Yaya's territory.

'At last he believes!' Yaya said solemnly. 'Doc knows that it was a ghost that rang the doorbell last night.'

But, seriously. If you were a ghost, would you ring a doorbell?

Father didn't really believe in ghosts and Yaya feared them but had never seen one. That left me as the family's ghost expert since it was me who'd seen Mother that night in the market, it was me who'd felt the ripple of electricity, the welling cold in the darkness.

I could tell them a thing or two about real ghosts.

And this definitely wasn't it.

All that day, Yaya had an alert look on her face, like a startled, pointy-eared dog. 'Did you hear that?' she cried every now and then. And several times she threw the front door open as if she wanted to catch someone sneaking around on the other side.

But there was never anybody there.

She pulled all the drapes shut, turning the house into a hot, dark oven.

Then, when she returned from shopping at the early morning market, she produced a baseball bat from her wicker basket stuffed with vegetables. A baseball bat!

'I will hide it here, OK?' She carefully positioned it just inside the living-room door. 'Just in case . . . we now have something to defend ourselves with.'

It was so ridiculous. What use would a baseball bat be against a ghost? You couldn't club a spirit with a bat even if you wanted to.

The bat behind the door made me feel uneasy. Would Yaya really pick it up, swing it high, and crack someone on the skull with it? Would *I*?

While she was busying with lunch, I hefted the bat from its hiding place, sneaked out into the back garden and dropped it into the dustbin.

I allowed a deep sigh to escape my lips. That's better. Now nobody had to fight anybody. Not that we had it in us to do so. Yaya was all bluster and no teeth. Father was too gentle and bookish. And me? I was a marshmallow masquerading as a potato.

I spent the day with a stupid smile on my face. I couldn't wait until the afternoon when Danny and I would be logged on again. It was like waiting until the last excruciating minute to unwrap a great big present.

After a bit of home school in the afternoon, I settled down with the laptop at last and checked on Danny's wall.

He had a new slogan up.

A friend indeed **shows up.**

Cheeky.
The laptop beeped.

> Hey, Rosa.

Hey, Rosa. Just like that, we were no longer Ansel95 and Stroppy and I felt . . . Happy? Bemused? Flattered? Frightened?

Awkward? Freaky? Creeped out?
My fingers stumbled on the keyboard:

> **Hey, Danny.**

Well. That didn't feel too weird. Just needed to try it out, I guess.

> Hey.

> **Hey.**

> Hey.

Not good. We could just hey each other for ever. Get a grip, Rosa! Say something.

> **Did you take any good photos yesterday?**

Nope. Too rainy.
Stayed home. Why?
Did something
interesting happen
in your parts?

Stayed home! Liar, liar, pants on fire!

I grinned at Danny's Mister Anybody profile picture. Two could play that game.

Nothing.

Nothing? Really?

NADA. NADA. NADA.

Is that Spanish?
What does that
mean?

NOTHING.

OK. Something's up.
You sound like a
ghost came and
rang your doorbell.

Bingo! He was definitely fishing.

Should I bite?

I stared at the screen, chewing my lip. Well. No time like the present.

Was it you?

Was it who?

Was it you who rang the doorbell?

Whose doorbell?

Stop it! I hate this game you're playing.

What game? I have no idea what you're on about. I thought we were friends, Rosa.

We ARE friends but . . .

If we're friends, why are you still pretending you don't live in Mirasol?

I DON'T!

You do. You know it and I know it. If we really were friends we would have met up a long time ago.

If we were friends we would have met up a long time ago.

My heart felt like it was going to burst right out of my chest.

I clenched my fists.

We could have met up a long time ago? And then what?

And then we wouldn't have been friends any more when Danny realized that his new friend was no ordinary girl. That the only sounds I could make were animal grunts. That I had a neck like chopped liver. That I was, in fact, a monster.

> Rosa! Are you still there?

My hands hovered over the keyboard but I snatched them away. Why did he have to push it? Why couldn't we stay the way we were?

> STROPPY!

I ran trembling fingers through my hair.

This was it. This was when we found out once and for all. Once we met, we would know if this was the beginning of a beautiful friendship or . . . the end.

> OK.

OK? OK WHAT?

OK, I WILL meet you.

Dang!

YES, I live on Mirasol.
YES, I will meet you.

Double dang!

That's why I was looking at
your pictures. I'd never seen
photos from our side of the
mountain. You do live on
this side of Banawa, don't
you?

Yes. In the village.

And you know where I
live.

I held my breath. Now was his chance to come clean. He'd been taking photos up and down our street.

The minutes ticked by. No reply. If I hadn't known better, I would have thought he'd logged off. When a bubble finally appeared on my screen, my heart was pounding so hard my chest ached.

> I don't know exactly where your house is . . . but I have a hunch it's the road at the far end of the island.

I stared at the quivering bubble. Why couldn't he just admit that he'd come to ring the doorbell?

> I'm a much better stalker than you. I'll tell you how I figured it out later.

Sure, OK. Tell me later.
If you're still around.

It was hot in the attic room but I cupped my icy hands and blew on my fingers to warm them up before I typed.

> So, yeah. Let's meet.

> Once you make up your mind, you don't waste time, do you?

> No time to waste.

> OK. Let's do it! How about next week . . . Monday?

I bit my lip.

> No, not Monday.

> How about the following Monday?

> No.

When, then?

After supper. Tonight.

17

Much later, I thought of how amazing it must have been for you, arriving in that magic city after the desolation of our life in Mirasol.

London with its spires, its knowing oldness, its absolute certainty. It was such a mixing bowl, churning with people of every colour, every story ever told, every word ever spoken. So easy to dive in, mix in, *disappear* into that melting pot. No fingers pointing, nothing to hide.

Kat, after you took that job in London, leaving me behind on the island, I thought of you every minute of the day. What is Kat doing now? I used to close my eyes and imagine that it was me striding down those gilded streets, me visiting museums and castles, me tending patients in your hi-tech hospital, me commuting on trains, me playing house in a compact little flat near work.

I allowed myself to write you *once* a week. Once. Even though every passing day my fingers itched to write another. I was stern with myself. Only once a week, Kara. That's all you're allowed. Filled my letters with foolish gossip. Is that film showing in England yet, are you following that TV series, did you read that book? What about that actress in that outfit? Light and breezy and uncaring.

Just once a week. More than that and I would have been saying too much, about the sameness of the island, the empty house, the empty street, the empty beach when I crept out like a thief to get some air and exercise. Going out to do my errands wearing a ridiculous scarf in the warmest weather, sitting alone in the cinema, avoiding contact with people, please, thank you, and then moving quickly on. Quickly. Quickly.

Out of sight.

Out of mind.

I didn't allow any of my emptiness to creep in. I wanted to match you, letter for cheerful letter.

Oh, I didn't want you to know how it really was. You were so excited, so bubbly, so happy to be in London. I didn't want to take that away from you.

Didn't want you to know how much I needed you.

Didn't want to give you that satisfaction.

We were apart for almost a year before you cracked.

YOU cracked.

It came just before Christmas, our first Christmas apart. Your letter fell through the mailbox and I felt a little thrill, like there was a current of energy emanating from inside the envelope.

Could that be possible? I knew even before I tore the envelope open that the message was going to be important.

Dear darling Kara, you wrote.

Life is so FULL in this country. I sit here in my little kitchen and listen to the buses rushing by on the road outside, so many people on the move. I sit here and I know that the theatre round the corner is filled with human beings, that schools, hospitals, restaurants and cafes – they are all buzzing. London just . . . TEEMS. It's amazing.

Sometimes I feel like a glass that someone's filling with water. Except the water pours and pours and never stops. You'd think that it would fill me up. But it doesn't. It's like there's something missing. You know all those stories of amputees who can still feel itching in their missing limbs? That's how I feel.

I think of you all the time, you know. I can't help it. What did we used to say? We're two halves of the same whole. Without each other we are incomplete. How could we ever imagine that we could live apart?

I've had enough of being alone. I love you, I miss you so much it hurts. I just can't do this any more – it's like I'm unable to get enough air. I can't live without you.

I've saved enough for your ticket. Don't say no. I should never have left you behind. I will never let us be apart again.

Please come to England. Be with me.

18

No. I couldn't wait.

If we waited, it was going to be unbearable torture wondering what he would think of me. Wondering whether he was going to take one look at me, scream with horror and run away?

I needed to know as soon as possible.

If he stayed, then we could get on with being friends.

If he left, I could get on with living without him.

TONIGHT?

Why not?
9pm. On the
promenade.

That feels . . . fast.

Why, are you worried about what you might find?

Of course not.

Have you got something to hide?

Be cool, dude.

Don't call me dude.

OK, then.

OK?

OK.

OK. 9pm. On the promenade.

> See ya later,
> alligator.

> So . . . do you
> admit it?

> Admit what?

> That you rang our
> doorbell last night.

> I admit nothing.

I hurried downstairs to my room and stood in front
of the dresser mirror, panting like I'd been running a
marathon.

I stared at myself. There was nothing monster-like
about the girl in the reflection. In jeans and T-shirt,
her dark hair spilling about her shoulders, she looked
like any teenager.

I pulled open the dresser drawer. Found a small
notebook and pen. Tucked it into my back pocket so
I wouldn't forget later. Hopefully Danny wouldn't

have any problems reading my handwriting. What was he going to say when he discovered I couldn't speak? I remembered Yaya's early days when she hadn't mastered sign language yet and couldn't make head nor tail of my baby writing. It was a real incentive to learn faster. But she was totally cool about it. Would Danny be different?

I was suddenly aware of butterflies fluttering violently in my stomach. No, not butterflies. Pterodactyls. Great, leathery, flapping dinosaur birds. I hugged my tummy. You will be fine, Rosa. Come what may.

I found a scarf down deep in the drawer and wrapped it round my neck.

With the scarf on, the girl in the mirror looked perfectly normal. She looked like Miss Anyone on her way to meet Mister Anybody.

I tried a smile. The face in the mirror lit up, the dark eyes glittering. The smile added a fierceness to the girl's expression. She looked a lot more confident than I felt.

She looked real enough.

She looked OK.

Danny would have to be a real jerk to reject me.

But what about Danny? Was *he* for real? What if it

turned out *he* weighed three tons, was prematurely bald and cross-eyed with dripping acne?

I swallowed.

But you like him, Rosa. So much. Even if he turned out to be the ugliest boy in the world, it wouldn't matter because you *LIKE* him. You can't fake personality.

And those photographs he was always posting. They were gorgeous. Someone who took photos like that had to be a good person, surely. You can't see beauty like that and be bad. You can't fake all that other stuff.

Can you?

Later, as I helped Yaya chop vegetables for dinner, it was hard to concentrate. I couldn't stop thinking about the night to come.

Thinking and worrying and exulting.

But Yaya was in a stranger mood than mine. She was like a flea, all over the kitchen, bouncing from one thing to another. 'Chop the carrots, oh no, do the potatoes first, is that pot boiling yet? The rice? The rice!' And all the while, it was like her eyes were attached to me with long, invisible ribbons, following my every movement. It was unnerving.

Finally she gathered herself up, cleared her throat and gave me a look. Oh no. I knew that expression on her face. I steeled myself.

'Why does your daddy insist on living here in Mirasol?' she said fiercely. 'The worst place in the world for someone with the Calm. You should be in a real school with boys and girls your age, not attending home school with only your boring old Yaya as a teacher. You should be spending too much money at the mall. Scaring yourself at a horror movie with your friends. Having your nails painted a ridiculous colour at a nail shop.'

As she spoke, she stood taller and taller until it felt like she'd doubled in height, eyebrows arched right up to her hairline.

What had brought this on? The doorbell incident? If Father had been here, he and Yaya would have had one of their discussions – if you could call talking at the same time while not listening a 'discussion'. Discussions that always ended with Father disappearing into his study in exasperation.

Yaya in her funny mood wouldn't stop. She just bashed on and on about London being the place for me. I was relieved when six o'clock came along and I could go upstairs, light my candles, sit and dream a little bit about my secret after-dinner date with Danny.

I stepped into the attic and my breath caught in my throat. I sensed it immediately. Something was missing.

I looked around the room, ticking boxes. Laptop on table, check. Poster on wall, check. Mother's picture in the frame, check. Candles on windowsill . . . gone.

That was why Yaya was in that weird mood. She'd taken away all the candles.

Rage swelled in my chest, a violent ocean.

'*AAAAH!*'

The sudden scream made me jump before I realized that it was coming from my own throat. STUPID Calm. STUPID twisted neck. I wanted to shout all the swear words I ever knew, shout foul hateful words. But *AAAAH* was all I could do. *AAAAH*. Useless, useless, USELESS!

I whirled towards the door, intent on barrelling my way downstairs to confront Yaya.

But I didn't have to. She'd followed me up the stairs.

Her pencilled brows were drawn together in a straight line. 'I'm sorry, Rosa,' she said in a firm, definitely unsorry voice. 'After last night, I thought it best to lose the candles.'

Lose the candles? Losing something implied a mistake, an accident . . . like losing a shoe under the bed or losing the remote control under a sofa cushion.

'*Ungh ungh ungh!*' I couldn't stop the ugly sounds grating out of my throat. My hands flew up, throwing angry words at Yaya in sharp, bitter shapes. But it was totally useless. Yaya's face was an expressionless mask.

'Enough is enough, Rosa,' she said softly. 'Those candles. They are so wrong! I told you before – it's unfair to the world of the spirits! Your mother will not be happy to be called back.' Then she said sorry again. 'I'm sorry, sorry, sorry.' She kept saying it, like a mantra. But she wasn't sorry, was she? She was *glad*. She'd always hated the thought of Mother coming back. She'd always been *afraid*. But why did she have to be afraid? The spirits were dead, weren't they? What could ghosts do to us? Maybe it was Mother she was afraid of. Maybe she just didn't want any COMPETITION.

The front door banged downstairs.

'Yaya? Rosa?' Father's voice drifted up to us. 'I'm home!'

I flung another dagger look at Yaya and whipped past her, practically flying down the steep staircase.

Even if Father didn't like the candles, he would back me up. Tell Yaya the candles did no harm. I could count on Father to feel guilty. Wasn't I his lonely, isolated child? He would only want to make me happy.

Inside me, a small girl threw back her head and bawled. *Mother! Mother! How are you ever going to find me now?*

When I got to the bottom of the stairs a gust of rainy weather struck me. The front door was open and a wet, salty breeze was blowing in. Father bustled past me with a stepladder under one arm and a drill in his hand.

What's that? But Father didn't see me signing. He was too busy positioning the ladder on the step outside the front door.

Next to his briefcase in the hallway was a large box. The label said: *Weatherproof Home Security Camera Kit with Monitoring Software for Phone and Computer.*

'You don't know how to install that,' Yaya said on the stairs behind me. She didn't sound at all surprised to see the camera kit.

Father rolled his eyes. 'Of course I do,' he said. 'If I can finish medical school, I can install CCTV. Besides, it comes with detailed instructions.'

'Where?' Yaya said. 'Where are the instructions? You haven't even opened that box.'

Father shrugged, glancing over his shoulder at her with that smug I-know-what-I'm-doing look he always had when he was doing DIY. His eyes settled on me and refocused.

'Oh, sweetie, I didn't see you there! I've got something here for you.'

How could he look at me and not see? He was so wrapped up in his own stuff he didn't notice the outrage on my face.

He clambered down from the ladder, reached into his briefcase and produced a small box. A mobile phone.

'This is for you, Rosa,' Father said. 'Enjoy.'

I stared dumbly at the picture of the mobile phone on the box. Who did Father think I would need to call?

Yaya patted me on the shoulder but I shrugged her hand off.

I signed, *But we've already got a phone!* On the wall of the kitchen. In fact, we never used it since neither Yaya nor I had any friends in the real world. Except, of course, when Yaya rang Father at work to nag him about his dinner getting cold on the table.

'But this one is just for you. This way you can text me if you need me. I'll show you how to text later when we set it up. I want you to be able to contact me without needing Yaya to talk on your behalf. In case of emergency,' Father said. 'Any emergency.'

I frowned. *Why?* I signed. *Why only now?*

'I . . . well, I have to admit the doorbell ringing last night got me thinking. I realized you were dependent on Yaya to get in touch with me if . . . well, if something happened. We can't be too careful, you know.'

I stared up at him. His eyes flickered then he looked away as if he was embarrassed.

Yaya clapped her hands. 'This is so good, so good, Doc. Now Rosa, we won't be so scared because we know Doc will come running in case we look out the window and see a burglar or even a ghost!'

I waited for Father to explode with laughter, waited for the snort of derision, waited for him to say, 'Stop your superstition, woman!' like he always did.

But instead he just nodded. 'Yes, text me. Text if you see anything, anything at all.'

19

After supper, Father and Yaya dived straight into battle over how the new security camera should be installed. Father crouched over the wiring in the hallway while Yaya hovered over him like a bothersome wasp, reading glasses on the tip of her nose, reciting from the manual, 'It says left to right! Why did you do right to left? No, not that screw. This one!'

They were totally engrossed, bickering over the drilling in the doorway, bickering over the wiring in the hall, and then bickering over the monitor in the kitchen.

Which was when I carefully wrapped my scarf round my neck and slipped out the front door.

The breeze blowing in from the sea smelled saltier as I picked my way along the side of the house and down the long sandy path to the beach, flanked by reedy sea grass. The air felt thick and wet and I closed my eyes briefly. Its cool touch on my skin felt good, washing away all my chaotic feelings.

My anger about the candles dwindled and stilled. Everything was going to be all right. How could it not be?

The black sky was covered with a skin of cloud, a soft liquid moon drifting in and out of the gaps. Whenever it shone clear, the concrete of the promenade ahead gleamed like a white ribbon. But everywhere else was just shadows.

It was so dark that when I looked in the distance I couldn't see the join of the horizon and the sky. The waves sighing on the shore were invisible to me.

Street lights stood along the promenade like soldiers in a shabby dress parade. At the end of the promenade the famous sign glowed under a lamp.

I was careful to stand just outside the light. It felt less exposed somehow.

The village twinkled like a cluster of tiny fireflies at the far corner. That was where Danny would be coming from.

But there was no sign of anyone.

Relax, Rosa. Perhaps he was taking extra care combing his hair. To impress me. I bit my lip. Perhaps I should have taken extra care with *my* hair. I suddenly wished I had a mirror.

But wasn't this the oddest turn of events? A few months ago, if you'd told me I would be meeting a strange boy on the beach at nine in the evening, I would have laughed like a drain. Me, out at night? Me and a *boy*? You must be joking!

Goosebumps rose on my arms, even though the breeze blowing from the sea was warm. I rubbed my arms until the bumps went away.

Of course, I was going to have to tell Father and

Yaya that I'd made a friend on the Internet. That I'd disobeyed every rule in the book about stranger danger.

Thinking of Yaya, my empty windowsill suddenly presented itself and hot anger surged in my stomach again. The *nerve* of her taking all my candles away! With all the fuss about mobile phones and CCTV I hadn't had a chance to talk to Father about it.

Tomorrow, Rosa, tomorrow. One thing at a time. Don't worry, Father will get your candles back. He wouldn't want you to be miserable – even if he doesn't believe in ghosts.

Ghosts! I glanced around involuntarily. All Yaya's whispered tales of lost souls and phantoms keeping step in dark alleys suddenly had my heart racing again. My hand crept into my jeans pocket, which was still full of Yaya's paranoid salt.

I yanked my hand out and shook myself. Silly Rosa. This is not the time to develop a fear of ghosts. You need to focus. Danny should get here soon. What are you going to say?

I pulled the pad out of my pocket.

Please don't be angry, I wrote. *I've got the Calm.*

Please don't be angry? Why should he be angry? I flipped to another page.

I've got the Calm. Sorry.

Too self-pitying.

I've got the Calm. Surprise!

Too flippant.

I wrote on page after page. But nothing I wrote seemed to strike the right note. And then the rain noises changed to a spatter and black spots appeared on the pages of my notebook. This wasn't just a wetness any more, but proper, earnest rain. I stuffed the pad back in my pocket and readjusted the scarf, winding it over my head and round my neck. Where was Danny?

There was a different quality to the rumble of the sea now, the steady splashing of the waves seemed to be separating into many individual noises.

Don't, Rosa. Don't pay any attention to it.

But I listened, closing my eyes. It sounded like . . . like voices. Murmuring. Calling.

Rain streamed on my head and I brushed the water impatiently from my eyes. Despite the tropical heat underlying the weather, I could feel a coldness welling in the pit of my stomach. My hands slowly turned into ice, great freezing shards at the ends of my arms.

Stop it, I scolded myself. You're frightening yourself. How many times had I myself told Yaya:

spirits can do NOTHING to you? They're DEAD! Yaya, didn't you yourself say that they're just souls in transit and the Earth is their waiting room?

The rain stopped. Turned itself off. And a sudden breeze whipped my hair over my eyes. I tossed it away, looking around me impatiently. Why wasn't Danny here yet? How long had I been standing here like a fool?

But the coldness was spreading throughout my body now. And then a trickle of electricity slowly rippled through me. I could feel it up to the roots of my hair. It felt just like . . . no, you must be imagining things, Rosa.

But that little tiny panicky voice was squeaking in the back of my head. You do know this feeling, Rosa. It's the same you had that night, many years ago in the market. When you saw Mother's ghost.

The whispering of the waves deepened. So many voices. All calling at the same time. I stared towards the shore.

Was it rain or some trick of the wind?

The blackness seemed to be moving.

I narrowed my eyes to slits, trying to blur everything, trying to pretend that there was nothing taking shape on the sand.

But it was there. A shadowy something. A someone. And it was walking slowly towards me.

The hairs rose on my arms. It's Danny, isn't it? But would Danny be so silent, so . . .

The shadow resolved. That wasn't a boy's shape. It had hair billowing and skirts blowing about. It was a woman.

My heart leaped in my chest like something on a spring. And the blood surged hot in my veins even as my teeth began to chatter.

She tilted her head, looking at me and then she began to hurry across the sand, her arms outstretched, the scarf wound round her neck fluttering like a flag.

I edged away from the bright pool of lamplight. All those years I'd planned what I would do when Mother's ghost finally came. How I would run to her, throw my arms round her. How I would take her hands in mine.

But I did none of those things.

I saw Mother and I ran away in terror.

20

My heart was an atom bomb. It detonated in my chest, *phwoom*, its mushroom cloud straining against my breastbone.

I couldn't breathe. But I kept running, the cold sweat burning my back, the tears streaking down my face.

As if in sympathy, the skies opened again. But this time it was like God had tipped a great bathful of water onto the Earth in one great gush. The skies poured on and on, harder and harder. By the time I'd struggled my way up to the house, there was a steeliness to the rain – it slashed at me like talons, the water cascading over my face and up my nostrils.

I stopped at the house, leaned my head on the breeze-block wall. Closed my eyes.

You coward, Rosa.

I tried to picture Mother walking slowly up the slope of the beach. Picking her way through the sand, her skirt blowing about her, arms held out gleaming in the street light's glow, hair whipping in the rising wind, the voices in the sea muttering louder and louder. I imagined the disappointed phantom, alone on the sand, one hand raised towards her unfaithful daughter. *Why are you running, Rosa? Don't you love me?*

It's unkind to summon the dead, Yaya kept telling me. And how I had mocked her. Ha-ha! You're just scared, Yaya. Scaredy cat!

Well, the last laugh was on me because now I was scared too. Now I understood what Yaya meant. Now I knew what it was like to be afraid.

I splashed my way up the rest of the path to the front door.

It was only when I was standing there, staring at the brass lock that I realized. I didn't have a key. But then there was a whirring noise and I became aware of a tiny pin-light of red above my head. Father's security camera.

The door swung open and I shrank back as Father loomed, his face contorted with anger.

But he pulled me quickly into the house, slammed the door shut and wrapped his arms around me.

He hugged me so fiercely I swear I could feel my ribs creaking. I felt a wetness trickling down my neck and realized he was crying. And if I hadn't been so shaken I would've laughed. Aren't you being a bit over the top, Father? But he made me feel better, he made me feel safe . . . so I just let him hug me until he held me away and began to rant in a hoarse voice, his eyes raw and red.

'You can't *do* that, you can't just leave the house without telling us! I thought something *terrible* had happened to you. I thought you'd been *taken*—'

Taken? What was he talking about? *Taken by whom?* I signed.

I felt like all the blood had receded from my face and I could hear my teeth chattering. I must have looked a fright. But Father was so engrossed in his own upset he looked right through me.

'*Taken! Or hurt! Or mugged! Or*—'

I threw my arms round him, pressing my cheek against his. His shoulders were like coiled wire, tight and tense. Poor Father. He did his best, didn't he? He didn't deserve another scare so soon after yesterday's doorbell event.

I wanted to say, *Father, I saw Mother. On the shore. She tried to speak to me. You were wrong about the spirits. You were wrong, there are such things as ghosts! Mother came. To me!*

But I couldn't tell him, could I? Because what did

I do when the moment I'd been waiting for all these years finally arrived?

I ran away.

I left Mother there, on the beach.

I clung to Father as if the world was about to end.

He leaned backwards, looking down at me, his eyes soft, cloudy blue with worry and love. 'I don't know what I would have done if something had happened to you,' he whispered. 'What were you doing out there, Rosa?'

I stared up into his sad face and guilt pierced deep into my chest. My signing came up small and full of remorse.

I needed air, my hands lied. *Needed to go out. Sorry, Father.*

The old Rosa would have said, *SHE'S OUT THERE. ON THE BEACH. MOTHER'S GHOST!* The old Rosa would have dragged Father out to the promenade. But I didn't want to go back. I was too afraid.

There was such relief in Father's eyes. 'I guess Yaya and I were being insufferable about the security camera,' he said ruefully. 'Sorry, sweetheart. We got a bit carried away. It's installed now. You won't have to think about it any more.'

He peered at me. 'You're looking exhausted,' he said, stroking the hair away from my forehead. 'I guess it's time for bed. Just . . . just don't take chances like that again. Next time, let me go with you . . . or take Yaya along.'

I nodded. Yaya's anxious face peeked in from the kitchen door. I smiled wanly at her and she opened the door wider, as if she was about to join us. But after all my deceit I just wanted to get away.

Going to bed now. Good night, I signed quickly.

Father nodded. *I love you*, he signed.

I bit my lip. *I love you too*, I replied.

He kissed the top of my head and let me go.

I rolled about restlessly on the bed, one thought melting into another. I should just tell Father and Yaya everything. About Danny, and about Mother on the beach. I had to. It would be like handing over a massive suitcase I couldn't carry any more, all my fear and my worry and my guilt. They were the grown-ups. Let them figure out what to do next.

But how do you sleep after something like that? I could hear every drop of rain, every rattle against the window, every thud on the floor.

Then I remembered where it all began.

Danny.

Danny never turned up. Danny was a no-show.

Disappointment sat on my chest like a boulder.

Well. That was that, wasn't it?

When the crunch came, Danny didn't deliver. He was just having a game with a girl on the Internet. Just like Father and Yaya warned.

Stranger danger. Danny had decided to be a stranger.

I laughed grimly.

Danny wasn't for real.

And Mother . . . Mother was for real, but I had run away.

21

Sleep wouldn't come and wouldn't come and wouldn't come.

I found myself glancing at the window, fearful that I might see ghostly fingers parting the curtains and Mother's disappointed spirit hovering there. *Why did you run away, Rosa? Why did you leave me?*

I screwed my eyes shut, wishing that slumber was a blanket I could simply pull over my head. Please, just let me sleep. I want to sleep.

And then at last I realized I was drifting into slumber, my body sinking deep into the mattress, my lids pressed tight over my eyes.

As I fell Yaya's voice began to whisper into my ear. 'Listen, Rosa, listen . . .' and I realized I'd begun to dream. 'Rosa . . . you like ghosts, yes? Well, you will like this one. This is a good ghost story.'

No! No ghosts! I didn't want to hear it! I knew this story – I'd begged Yaya to tell it often enough. But not now. Please, not now. I thrashed and tried to wake myself up again, but there was no stopping it. The story was telling itself whether I wished it or not.

Oooh, Rosa, this story is probably true because Mrs Santos, my librarian at primary school, told it to me and a librarian would never lie, yes?

Mrs Santos and her husband bought a house down the road from our school. It was an amazing buy – so cheap, and yet it had a pretty garden and a beautiful kitchen with large windows.

If they felt a tiny change in the atmosphere when they entered the house, a kind of tightening and a slight drop in the temperature, they shrugged it off as stress. Who wouldn't be a little bit stressed when purchasing property?

It was only when they had done the deal, moved in, that they realized that there was something in the kitchen.

(Are you scared yet, Rosa? No?)

There was something in the kitchen. Something angry. The walls throbbed with some kind of energy, the air was spiky with . . . with irritation. You walked into the kitchen and you could feel the fury of it, hot and strange. Things moved of their own accord. Cutlery shook in the drawers. Pots dropped from their hooks. Cupboard doors banged open and shut.

The kitchen was haunted.

Mrs Santos searched old newspaper archives and found an article about her new house. There had been a double murder. The killer had only planned to kill the husband. But he had run into the wife in the kitchen and shot her too.

Mrs Santos had a friend named Anna, a medium who could speak to the dead. She asked Anna for help. How could she rid the kitchen of this malevolent ghost?

Anna explained that ghosts who haunt a single spot are trapped spirits. They are literally suspended in a single moment, a fragment of time, condemned to relive the emotion of that moment over and over again for ever and ever. The ghost has no sense of time passing, no sense of the living world, no sense of its own deadness.

The solution, Anna said, was simply to let the ghost know – tell the ghost it is dead. Once it realizes that it no longer belongs to this world, it would be freed to leave and find peace.

Relieved, Mrs Santos invited Anna to come and do the telling. Anna had much experience with ghosts, she could get it over with quickly, send the ghost off post-haste so that Mrs Santos and her husband could get on with enjoying their new house.

(Are you relieved, Rosa? Well, just you wait . . .)

Remember what I said about candlelight and ghosts? How the flicker reminds a spirit of its human heartbeat? Well, Anna came with many candles. She lined them up on the floor, along the walls, and up on the kitchen counters on the tiles. She switched off all the electricity in the kitchen, even the fridge, so that the spirit would not be distracted by other energies but would listen only to her.

And then she lit all the candles, drew the curtains, sat down at the kitchen table with Mrs Santos and waited.

The ghost appeared almost immediately.

It was a fury of energy, the glimmering shape of a woman. She paced the kitchen floor, back and forth, back and forth. She didn't see the two women sitting at the table, so preoccupied was she with her pacing, her hands gathered in fists, her head bent. She hurried to the window, looked out, shook her head and began pacing again.

'Excuse me,' the medium said softly.

The spirit glanced up, irritated. 'What is it?'

'Why are you pacing?'

The spirit glanced at the watch on her ghostly wrist. 'I'm waiting. He's late. He's always late.'

'Who are you waiting for?'

The spirit whirled angrily towards the medium, and even though the weather was tropical-hot they felt the stirring of a frosty breeze. 'My husband!' she snapped. 'I'm waiting for my husband.'

'You don't know!' Anna breathed. 'Your husband was shot!'

'What!' The spirit stopped pacing and glared at her. 'Who are you? Why are you saying this to me?'

'I am sorry,' the medium said. 'Your husband is not coming. He is dead.'

The spirit clutched at her throat. 'No! It cannot be true!'

'He died a long time ago,' Anna whispered.

'No!' The spirit began to weep. 'Why are you telling me this?' she groaned. 'Oh, why?'

'You need to know,' Anna said, 'because you need to find peace.'

'Why? What peace can I find if my husband is dead?'

'You need peace, because you are dead too.'

And Mrs Santos leaned forward, expecting to see the spirit's eyes widen, expecting her to slowly evaporate into nothing and free the house of her presence for ever.

But no such thing happened.

The ghost stopped weeping, glaring at Anna and Mrs Santos at the kitchen table. And then she began to scream, high and piercing with anguish and rage. And the kitchen erupted in a volcano of flying things. The windows exploded, broken glass suddenly showering the room, the light fixtures writhing, sparking coils of wire, ripped from the ceiling, doors torn from cupboards, the knife block hurled to the floor, knives shooting everywhere like deadly missiles.

Anna and Mrs Santos only just managed to stumble out of the kitchen to the safety of the garden.

The spirit didn't want peace. She stayed in the room, raging, destroying everything. Anna tried using the salt she'd taken along for protection. She quickly opened the door and threw the sack of salt in. The bag exploded on contact with the floor, sending salt flying to all corners of the kitchen.

But it was not enough. The ghost was impervious. They would have needed all the salt in the ocean to vanquish its angry spirit.

Mrs Santos never did live in the house nor did she ever manage to sell it. She and her husband simply abandoned it and moved into an apartment on the other side of the school.

The house stands there still, alone on its road, derelict and empty. Save for the storming of the malevolent spirit in the kitchen, refusing to accept that she's dead. And still waiting for a husband that is never going to return.

It was the pounding of my heart that jolted me awake. Or maybe it was the fact that my nightie was soaking with cold sweat.

I turned my face into the pillow and waited for the violence in my chest to ease.

Whenever Yaya had told that story, we drew the curtains, turned off all the lights and huddled in bed together, enjoying the story's delicious shocks and terrors.

There was nothing delicious about it now.

My brand-new mobile phone lay on the bedside table. The clock display blinked green.

00:30 a.m.

Half past midnight.

Then I heard it. A distant thud. It came from downstairs.

I climbed out of bed and peered out my door. A

soft glow emanated from the bottom of the stairs. Someone was down there. I tiptoed quietly to Father's door. Knocked softly, then pushed it open.

Father wasn't in his bed. Right. It was just Father making all that noise downstairs. He always went down when he couldn't sleep. He called it Old Man Insomnia. Happened to all men beyond middle age, he said. Sleepy before midnight, up before sunrise. Couldn't be helped. He'd long ago stopped fighting it. Whenever he found himself awake in the small hours, he simply got up and went downstairs to read or watch TV or catch up with some work, hoping that sleep would come again at some point.

Well, I couldn't sleep either. I didn't fancy facing up to another nightmare and the thought of cuddling up with Father on the sofa appealed.

I padded down the stairs.

The soft rumble of snoring floated out of the living room.

Father was *asleep*! I stifled a giggle. So much for Old Man Insomnia.

I pushed the door open and crept in.

Father lay asprawl on the sofa in a white vest and faded blue pyjama trousers, his head thrown back, his snores rumbling deep and steady. His briefcase lay open on the occasional table, books and papers scattered everywhere.

The TV screen crackled with white noise. Whatever he was watching had long gone off the air. On his knee a heavy medical tome lay open, and in his hand he clutched a postcard.

Poor Father. I approached on tiptoe, knelt next to him and carefully slid the book off his lap and put it on the table. He muttered something but didn't wake.

I carefully took the postcard from his hand and he sighed as if a great weight had been taken off his shoulders.

It was a photo of one of those bright red, double-decker London buses. It had a British stamp on it, the one with the Queen's head. Tall, slanting handwriting covered the entire card. The handwriting looked familiar somehow. I'd seen it before. The date at the very top was 15 October. That was just two days ago. Probably from one of his old colleagues in London.

I read the message.

And suddenly my heart was exploding in my chest again, and goosebumps were pimpling all over my arms. I dropped the card as if it was suddenly crawling with maggots. It lay on the floorboards like a dead thing, but the words continued to swim, taunting, in front of my eyes.

Jon
We'll be together again soon, my darling. I'm coming.
Please don't push me away. Take me back.
I love you.
K

22

I whirled round to a picture frame on a side table. It was a photo of me as a baby in Father's arms. Written across the bottom of the photo in Mother's handwriting was *Jon with Rosa, eight months old*, the words tall and slanting. Just like on the postcard.

I lowered myself slowly into the chair opposite Father. A huge ball of ice was growing in my tummy, turning all the blood and slime and bile in my organs into a cold, slushy mass.

The handwriting was everywhere in the house. Scribbled on photos. Scribbled all over that album of mementoes of my birth: *Weight: 8 lbs 3 oz. Time of Birth: 4 a.m.!!!* On that photo of me and Mother on my bedside table: *To Jon, Happy Father's Day, With all our love, K and R*

K for Kara. Mother was alive.

It was not a ghost, there on the beach. It really was Mother. She was alive.

And all this time, Father knew. I looked at the

card again. *Please don't push me away.* He'd sent her away?

What could have driven them apart? I searched my memories. Had I missed something? Had they been fighting? Did they not love each other? Why would Father send her away?

But all I could remember were happy, loving scenes of Mother and Father together.

I closed my eyes. Oh my God. I remembered the box of Mother's ashes, heavy as a brick on my knees. Father had pretended to scatter her ashes in the ocean. What sort of sick game had he been playing?

He had lied about her death. Did he really plan to lie to me all my life?

Father's eyes opened, and at the sight of me he smiled softly. 'Oh, hello, sweetie. Why are *you* up?' He yawned, licked his lips and stretched, dislodging a stack of documents so that they cascaded to the floor in a flapping paper flutter.

I heard the click of his knees as he sat up.

A whole minute ticked slowly by before he actually looked at me properly, followed the downward glance of my dead eyes and saw.

'No!' He lunged across the table, snatched the postcard from the floor and began ripping it to pieces, tearing each shred into smaller shreds until the table between us was covered with tiny crumbs of card.

I still couldn't move. But the heat of my anger was melting away the ice now, and my tummy began to revolt. As if I'd swallowed some terrible toxin that it had to expel immediately. I clapped my hands over my mouth and ran out to the bathroom in the hall.

I fell on my knees, elbows on the toilet seat, retching into the bowl until there was nothing left to heave.

'Rosa.' Father was behind me. He took a hand towel, wet it at the sink and began to press it against my face.

I snatched it from him. I didn't need his sympathy. I could look after myself.

'Rosa, it's not what you think. It's not from Mother.'

I threw the towel on his chest. It made a sharp, wet, whip-cracking sound.

That is Mother's writing. My hands shook as I signed.

'No, no, no.' He leaned on the wall as if he didn't trust his legs to hold him upright. 'You don't know what really happened.'

You've been LYING to me!

He reached out and tried to take me in his arms. But the feel of his hands disgusted me. I struggled, smacking his hands away, and ran out of the bathroom into the hallway.

He followed, trying to grab my wrists, but I pulled away. And slapped him across the face.

I hit him so hard his face snapped to the side and tears popped out of his eyes.

But I didn't care.

You sent Mother away! I signed. *She wants to come back!*

'No, Rosa! Never! Give me a chance to explain!'

Father finally managed to get a hold of my wrists so that I couldn't sign. He didn't want me to throw the truth at him. He just wanted to shut me up. I cried out, thrashed about, tried to rip myself away. But his fists were as hard as manacles.

He manoeuvred me towards the sitting room, perspiration glittering on his forehead. 'Shhh, shhh,' he hushed over the horrid noises shrilling from my twisted throat. '*Listen*, you must listen.'

But he never got the chance.

We both heard it at the same time.

A dull thud on the front door.

We both stopped and listened.

The sound of shuffling feet outside the front door was unmistakeable.

Our eyes met, and all I could think was Mother. Mother, you've come, Mother. But in Father's eyes there was an awful horror. As if a corpse had scraped itself out of the ground and dragged its putrid, maggoty limbs all the way up to our front door.

And then . . .

Bang! Bang! Bang!

The door's wooden panels quaked under the pounding.

Father's skin was now drained of all colour – he might as well have been one of the ghosts that he loathed so much. He stared at me with haunted eyes.

I leaped to my feet and he lunged to stop me.

'No! For God's sake, don't open the door, Rosa!'

But I was already fumbling with the latch, not caring that my throat was squawking in excitement. *'Ungh! Ungh! Ungh!'*

It was Mother, wasn't it?

Why else would Father be so afraid? She'd come at last and he still didn't want me to discover the lie we'd been living.

I unfastened the latch. Pulled open the door.

But it wasn't Mother.

On our front step stood a teenage boy. He sagged like wet laundry flapping on a washing line, only staying upright because he was clinging to the top of the door frame with one long arm. A bruise was purpling under one eye and blood trickled down his temple, lumping up on the piercing shaped like a safety pin on his eyebrow.

He had a nosebleed too, the blood smeared all over his mouth like strawberry jam.

And yet he grinned at me as if his appearance was one big joke. The bleary eyes twinkled and he actually winked.

He looked over my shoulder and held out a hand for Father to shake. But the movement unbalanced him and he toppled down to the floor.

I stared down at him, mouth open.

A Friend Indeed Shows Up.

And here he was.

Father threw himself down on the floor beside him.

'Danny!' he cried. 'What on earth are you doing here?'

23

Father knew Danny?

Danny's eyelashes fluttered open. His eyes were glassy but they slowly refocused and he grinned. His hands moved. He was signing.

Hello, Doc. Then his face twisted, his head fell back and his mouth opened, gasping for breath.

'Dammit, Danny.' Father scowled. His hands scrabbled at Danny's neck and I realized that he was unknotting the dirty white neckerchief that the boy wore round his neck. As it came off, the hairs prickled at the back of my neck.

Monsters are in the eye of the beholder.

The welts on his neck were rougher than mine, the skin jaggedy and so reddish that at first glance it would be easy to think that someone had cut his throat.

Danny collapsed backwards, his eyes rolling into his eyelids.

I shook Father's shoulder, signing frantically. *What happened?*

But Father shook his head, 'He's fainted. I think he'll be OK.' He frowned down at Danny, muttering. 'What sort of trouble are you in now, boy?'

I stared at the boy on the floor. He had one safety-pin piercing on his eyebrow and one in the cartilage of one ear. He wore shabby black jeans so threadbare they hung around his knees in shreds. His black T-shirt was caked brown with dirt. He looked sticky and wet. I sniffed. He smelled like he'd been swimming in an unflushed toilet bowl.

'Jesus Mary Joseph!' Yaya appeared sleepily at the top of the staircase in a pink bathrobe. 'Who is this? What's going on?' She stared at the boy, her mouth open and closing soundlessly at first before she wrinkled her nose. 'Pah! Stinky!'

'Yaya, come,' Father commanded without looking. He put his ear against Danny's chest, listening.

Yaya inched down the stairs, eyeing Danny as if he was a rodent that had appeared in the larder. 'One of your patients?'

Father nodded tersely.

But realization had dawned. Yaya's eyes were staring. At the piercings. At the shredded trousers. *'Jesus Mary Joseph! You TOLD him where we lived? You LET HIM COME TO OUR HOUSE?'*

'YAYA!' Father barked. And then he seemed to recover his composure, holding his hands up. 'No, no, Yaya! I didn't. But he found out somehow. Now *please* help.'

Father took Danny's head and shoulders and Yaya gingerly took his greasy legs. I did my best to help lift somewhere in the middle. Yaya made vomiting noises at the back of her throat as we lifted.

It was an effort. He looked skinny but he weighed a ton.

We stumbled to the sitting-room sofa, Yaya shrieking a little as we clumsily squeezed through the door from the hall. We put him down on the sofa and Danny's head flopped back with a slapping noise.

I let go of his shirt. My hands were disgusting with slime and grit and mud.

'Ugh!' Yaya was examining her own hands. 'Rosa, come, we must wash!'

She ushered me to the bathroom, standing over me as I lathered my hands with soap. She didn't have to monitor how thoroughly I cleaned myself, I scrubbed and soaped and scrubbed as if I wanted to rid my hands of every speck of dirt, every trace of DNA even that might have transferred from Danny.

I turned my face away. I didn't want her to see the upset on my face. I could feel my lips wobbling, my cheeks burning with shame.

None of this was an accident, was it?

Father knew Danny. Danny knew Father.

The joke was on me.

When we returned from the bathroom, Father had taken Danny's shoes off and was in the process of pulling his T-shirt off.

I gasped. A tattoo of a massive snake wriggled across one shoulder blade and down one arm. I'd glimpsed a tattoo or two in his photographs but the real thing still came as a shock. For a moment, I thought Father was going to take Danny's trousers off too, but to my relief he didn't. The boy's torso was a paler shade of brown than his face and he had more tattoos on his chest and back, lizards and spiders and things with staring eyes. Purple bruises blossomed underneath all the tattoos like someone really clumsy had attempted to colour them in.

What happened to him? I asked Father.

'Looks like he was beaten up.' Father shook his head. 'Danny's been in trouble before. Refuses to be more careful. Keeps taking risks. Look at those tattoos. It's a wonder he managed to have them done and not be discovered. His parents have been beside themselves.'

'That boy is bad news,' Yaya clucked. She fetched some towels from the bathroom, tucking them under Danny to protect the sofa from his filth.

'Maybe you could put a towel over him as well?' Father suggested mildly.

Yaya threw a large towel over the boy, with a pained expression on her face. 'The sofa covers will need washing tomorrow.'

'Yaya.' Father scowled. 'Forget the hygiene for a moment. Give him a break, he's just a kid.'

We all stared at the unconscious boy.

Father turned to look at me. He had his soulful, doggy eyes on, begging me to understand.

Danny's appearance had interrupted our big confrontation. There was so much he needed to explain, so many lies he needed to right. But he didn't say anything. Now wasn't the time. Not in front of Danny and Yaya. Especially Yaya. She would go crazy on us – she was already freaked out enough about ghosts and Danny's dramatic entrance. And Father's betrayals would certainly lose him all her respect. Like he'd lost mine.

I dropped my eyes, avoiding his gaze.

He fetched the first-aid kit from the bathroom and began to clean the cut on Danny's forehead with antiseptic. As he worked, he talked softly about Danny, his story punctuated by impatient sighs and huffing from Yaya.

'He was so small when he came to the clinic for the first time. One of those skinny little things, big blinking eyes with a fringe of black hair hanging over them, and a huge smiling mouth.'

I stared at Father as he talked. There was a small smile twitching on his lips as he remembered meeting Danny for the first time, a little boy with the personality of a planet. 'Couldn't sit still, couldn't stop signing, his hands waving like windmills.' Father actually chuckled at the memory, and then his eyes flicked sideways at me.

He looked . . . he looked guilty. For the first time he was telling me about the life he led outside our world. I had always thought Father's work was . . . well, work. Not people. Not charming children that he looked forward to seeing every check-up. For the first time, I realized I was not the only person Father cared about.

'I'd never met a child like him,' Father was saying.

'He wouldn't stop asking questions. And I couldn't help myself. I made extra time with him so that I could answer everything he asked. When he asked why the chair squeaked, I told him about the mechanics of springs and friction and sound. When he asked what I was writing on my pad, I read it out loud to him. When he asked where I was born, I brought a little globe to the clinic so that at his next check-up I could show him that England was on the other side of the world.'

I remembered that. Because it was my globe. When it had vanished from my room, I had been inconsolable. It had reappeared again the next day and Yaya had acted like it had returned by magic.

I felt a tiny stab of pain in my chest, so sudden that I almost cried out. I looked away from Danny, looked at the wall, at the sofa, at the picture of Mother on the side table. Suddenly I couldn't bear the sight of Danny. Suddenly Father seemed a stranger who had another life that didn't include me. I was jealous.

Father finished dressing the cut on Danny's forehead and began to clean the mess off the rest of him with the bowl of water, soap and face towel that Yaya had fetched from the bathroom. He cast a glance at the clock softly glowing on the wall.

It was three a.m.

'I think you guys had better go to bed,' he said. 'I'll look after Danny.'

Yaya hid a yawn behind her hand. 'Go on, then, Rosa. Bedtime.'

I looked at Father. He still sat on the edge of the sofa next to Danny, his eyes pleading. Mother was outside on the beach, I wanted to tell him. She's out there, somewhere. Why won't you let her come home, Father? What happened between the two of you?

He held open his arms.

So he wanted to act like nothing had happened between us. Like this humongous betrayal of not telling me Mother was alive was not going to change anything.

I could play Father's game. I didn't want Yaya to notice that anything was askew, either.

I went and gave him a hug, pulling away quickly. But Father held on, whispering in my ear.

'We will talk later, Rosa, OK?' I turned my head to look into his face. He smiled and it made him look so loving, so honest, so *innocent*. I glared at him.

Father let me go.

'*Ungh ungh ungh!*'

It was a deep grating noise. Yaya and I whirled round.

Danny was awake.

He opened his mouth as if he was going to say something. But he couldn't, of course. His hands flapped up to sign something.

The hands suddenly curled up in claws on his chest. His legs kicked and the lamp on the side table toppled off with a crash.

'Oh my God,' Father cried.

Danny's body was ramrod straight. His eyes rolled up in their sockets and he began to shake uncontrollably.

All those years of practising for the Calm and wondering if an emergency would ever happen – and here it was. I gaped. I'd never seen anything like it.

Father scrabbled in the first-aid kit and pulled out an injector.

'Hold still, Danny,' Father said, clamping a hand on Danny's chest even as he tried to adjust the injector.

But Danny wouldn't hold still. He began to thrash, arms and legs stiff and stabbing, uncontrollable.

Yaya leaped onto Danny and tried to pin his shoulders down so that Father could give him the injection. But Danny was strong. One unruly swipe of his arm and Yaya tumbled backwards.

'Dammit, Danny.' Father was really struggling. I threw myself across Danny's chest and held him down with my body weight. Yaya sat down on his legs. 'Hang on,' Father muttered, pressing the injector into Danny's thigh, right through the denim of his trousers.

Danny's body jerked as if Father had thrust a knife into him.

'One elephant . . . two elephant . . . three elephant . . .' We all counted. This was it. How many times had we practised in case of emergencies?

The boy gasped as the medicine took effect, his body arching and then falling limp.

I levered myself off his chest.

'I've got to take him to the hospital. Right now!' Father cried.

There was a steely set to his jaw as he slipped an arm under Danny's shoulders and lifted him up. He half dragged, half carried Danny's limp body (still clad only in jeans) to the door, all the while shouting, 'Open the front door, Rosa. Yaya, where are the car keys?'

Before he manhandled Danny out into the rain, he turned to Yaya. 'I will get back as quickly as I can. Lock the door, Yaya. Don't let anyone in. LOCK THE DOOR!'

And then they were gone.

24

I t was sunny in London. *That* surprised me.

You read all the things people say about English weather, brollies, stiff upper lips, and you hear that song about a foggy day in London – then what do you find? Blue skies, bright yellow daffodils, glinting spires. I had imagined all the olde worldy stuff, the cobbles and grand buildings and mossy statuary, fountains, pillars. But in my imagination, it was all lit low, like a black and white film, with long shadows and a veil of rain over everything, lacy and grey.

Sunshine was the last thing on my mind.

There you were at the airport, waiting right at the gates. And seeing you there – familiar, beloved, your face open, tears of joy streaking your cheeks, your smile like the sun, brilliant, blazing – it shook me to the core, Kat.

I'd been pretending for months that I was OK without you, that I didn't miss us being together. But it was a lie.

Your leaving had gouged a hole in me, wide open, weeping like an infected wound, desperate to be filled.

We embraced tightly, like we were trying to fuse into one

another, two sisters becoming one. Hugging and hugging. In my mind vines grew and twined around us, binding us closer and closer. We had to make up for putting that ocean between us. Never again, never again.

It felt so good, Kat. And I wondered then if all twins were like this, if all twins needed this physical closeness. Our coming together revealed to me what a terrible time our separation had been.

My vines wound round and round, and when we broke apart, smiling and wet-eyed and a bit embarrassed what with everyone at the airport staring and grinning, I was surprised.

I thought that would do it. We were together again. That would fill the hole.

But it didn't.

Once we were in the quiet of your flat, Papa and Mama smiling in your gilt frame, a map of Mirasol on the wall, our photos as baby twins in pride of place on the mantelpiece; once we'd put away my things, turned up the heating for my sake, thrown a blanket over my knee; once you'd shown me how everything worked and made me a cup of tea just because that was the British thing to do, even though I didn't want one . . . only once we'd done all that did I notice.

You'd changed, Kat.

One year apart had its effect on me, but I couldn't say that it had altered me much. But you. The year had definitely changed you.

Growing up together, sleeping under the same sheet, wearing matching pyjamas, matching T-shirts, blowing birthday candles out at the very same moment, all those years of being you and me, inseparable and the same.

OK, I admit that when we were growing up I was the bossy one. When Mama asked, 'What happened here? Who did this?' I could see you looking sideways at me, waiting, letting *me* decide how we would respond. I led and you followed. You didn't mind, did you, Kat? That was just the way of things.

Now, when I looked at the lift of your chin, the square of your shoulders – you seemed so . . . free. The way you walked, the swing of your hips, the sureness of you. All those years when it was Kara and Kat, Kat and Kara . . . they just tumbled away. You were a woman with your own life now, your own thoughts, your own future.

And you looked at me as if you knew something I didn't.

You took the week off from work so that we could do some tourism, so that you could settle me in. We did London in overdrive. The Tower of London. The Houses of Parliament. Westminster Cathedral. All the galleries. All the museums. We saw *everything*.

And I watched you. Observed the little changes that added up to . . . well, someone else.

But you have to understand, little sister, I didn't resent it.

No, no, of course not.

I *liked* the new you. The new you was fabulous, confident, more sophisticated. Cool.

What I missed was who we used to be *together*.

Then you went back to work.

It takes time, I suppose, to get used to normal. Normal in London was nothing like normal in Mirasol, of course. No more hiding, much more doing. Get on with it. Get going.

Meanwhile you were out all day, except some Fridays and Mondays when you got home early enough for a whirl around the shops or the cinema. But mostly you were home late, tired. But I didn't mind, honest, Kat, I was just happy to be in London with you.

And then one day you came home early and before you'd even opened your mouth, I knew something was up. It was in the way you looked at me, slantways, in the blush that slowly tinted your cheeks.

What? I signed. *What's the matter?*

'I . . . I'm going out tonight. I hope you don't mind.' That blush was still spreading! Oh, look at it blooming on your neck.

Where to? I signed. And I was not being nosy, honest.

I just wanted to know.

And then you burst into tears and I was even more baffled than before.

Why are you crying?

'Oh, Kara, someone's asked me out. He's one of the doctors at the hospital. I didn't have the courage to tell you about him. Do you mind?'

You looked so embarrassed, Kat. How silly of you to even think twice.

Of course I don't mind! Why should I mind?

Oh, but we had a lovely evening, getting you ready. This was how I'd always imagined sisters would be. Normal sisters. Doing each other's hair and nails. Picking out clothes.

I was so excited for you. How I teased you as I blow-dried your beautiful black hair, combed it until it was a slippery shiny thing, picked out a shade of pink lipstick that brought out the lustre of your complexion. And then you insisted on doing the same to me, and we primped and combed and laughed and it was the best time. The best.

We sat, side by side in front of the dresser mirror, smiling and marvelling at ourselves. And then a shadow passed over your face and you turned to me.

'I . . I didn't tell you everything, Kara.'

I raised an eyebrow. I'd thought you more confident,

more sophisticated. But tonight you were your old self, my anxious little sister, desperate for my approval in everything she did.

'He's a specialist.'

I rolled my eyes. Did you really think this was an earth-shaking revelation?

'A specialist of the Calm.'

I frowned. Why would you keep that from me? I looked away, trying to compose my face. No wonder you were consumed with such guilt. Did it matter, though? It didn't matter, did it?

'I attended a talk about the Calm at the hospital. I wanted to know if there was anything else we could do, you know? For you. And he was very good. So eloquent and caring. Such a good speaker. And afterwards I went up to talk to him.'

You told him about me? What did he say?

And you blushed again, Kat. Right to the roots of your hair. I could see it.

'I didn't.'

I stared at you.

'I didn't tell him about you.'

I sat very still, just looking. Then I pushed my hands between my knees, afraid they might fly up and say something to ruin our lovely afternoon together. Wouldn't *you* think that odd, Kat? Not mentioning that your sister had the Calm to a specialist?

That lonely wound ached inside me.

'I . . . Well, I was going to but . . . the way he looked at me, you know, we kind of . . . fell into talking about other things.'

And then it wasn't loneliness I felt any more, Kat. Suddenly there was a sour taste in the back of my throat. I looked at your smooth hair, your velvety cheek.

All right, I admit it. I was jealous.

'I . . . I feel embarrassed about it now,' you laughed. And you threw your arms around me, kissed me on both cheeks, held me close. 'I don't know what came over me. I was just . . . it was just . . . well, he was very nice, you know? Will you ever forgive me, Kara?'

Of course, I signed. *No problem.*

We picked a blue dress. Royal blue. It made your caramel skin glow, and showed off the darkness of your hair. It clung lovingly to your slim figure. Too lovingly. When the doorbell rang we were still struggling to get you into it.

On the third ring, you waved me away, 'Go get the door, Kara, say hello. Just one more second and I'll be done.'

I raced to the door and threw it open, panting a little from our exertions.

I only had the briefest impression of someone tall with broad shoulders and an untidy thatch of sandy hair before I was swept up in a bold embrace.

He pressed against me, his lips moving against mine, and I pushed away, clapped my hand over my mouth, eyes like platters.

'*Ungh ungh ungh!*'

He stared at me, confused. 'Kat?'

'Jon?' You were right behind us.

And Jon, mouth open, stared at you, so gorgeous in your blue dress ... and at me, dishevelled in jeans. His eyes darted between you and me before settling on the scarf wound round my neck. And he knew instantly, of course, that I had the Calm. He saw patients every day in his clinic. He knew.

He sputtered, 'I thought ... I thought ...'

I couldn't help it, Kat, I began to laugh. That will teach you not to warn people that you had a twin sister! You should have known! You can't erase me at the first sign of a nice-looking young man!

He grinned bashfully at me.

But *you* didn't smile, Kat. Oh, no. Your mouth straightened out into a pink line and you tossed your hair over one shoulder. 'I'll explain later, Jon,' you said tightly. 'We'd better go, it's getting late.'

And as you both went out the door, you flashed me a backwards look. Oh, I will always remember that look. Because wasn't that where it all began? Wasn't that the moment when everything changed?

I shrugged and turned away, still giggling. Looking back now, I had no idea. No idea that something had broken that night. Something we would never be able to fix.

25

Something clattered to the floor when the door shut behind Father and Danny. Plaster again. I looked up. Cracks spidered all over the ceiling. It was slowly falling apart and it was the first time I'd realized how bad it was.

'Come on, Rosa. To bed.' Yaya drew her pink bathrobe close around her and with one hand on my shoulder began to steer me up the stairs, talking all the while.

'That boy, Rosa! Ridiculous-looking! Safety pins in his ears! He could have died you know! Made a mess of the sofa. I'll have to wash all the covers now. They're going to shrink to nothing! And your Father. It's morning already! How is he going to run his clinic later? He hasn't had any sleep!'

And on and on. She just wouldn't shut up but I didn't mind. We were both still fizzing from the nervous energy of the past night, and it was as if she was trying to get rid of all that electricity. Her chatter filled the empty house, filled the air, filled my head up like a balloon fills up with air, pushing everything else out so I didn't have to think.

She walked me to my room, arm now round my shoulders. She must have been tired. The floor was thick with clothes I'd thrown down when I undressed earlier. But not a single *tsk* did I hear.

I climbed into the bed and she sat down on the side, still rabbiting: 'You can get up late tomorrow. That boy will be fine, don't worry. I can call the hospital first thing when I get up and check how they are. I always wake up early, don't I? What do you want for lunch?'

I listened sleepily, not wanting her to stop, not wanting her to leave me alone with spectres on my mind.

Stay? I signed.

'Jesus Mary Joseph, you baby!' she cried. But she promptly climbed under the sheet with me, still scolding and complaining. I lay my head on her terry-pink shoulder and threw an arm over her soft little potbelly, letting her endless continuing patter fall around me like a soft shower.

But even with Yaya's comfort, my mind wouldn't stop. I dreamed that I was in the sitting room, groping in the dust, sifting through the scattered shreds of postcard until I found the one with K on it. K for Kara. Mother. And in my mind, I fanned all the tiny pieces out on the floor, sorting and rearranging until the words leaped out.

Don't push me away. Take me back.

And then I was back on the promenade, craning to see someone in the shadows shifting on the black shore. Mother? Are you here then, Mother? But why didn't you follow me back? Where are you now?

'It's not her!' Father had cried when he saw the postcard. But still I searched. Not Mother? But how could that be?

I saw her, didn't I?

Didn't I?

Ding dong.

I rolled over but something caught in my sheet jerked me to a stop. I opened one eye.

Yaya lay with my sheet somehow wound tightly around her. She made a purring noise every time she exhaled through her teeth. A sheen of sweat glowed on her forehead. I could see the whites of her eyes peeking from under her lashes. I smiled. She was unwakeable when she was this asleep. No way was she keeping her promise to get up early!

The room was boiling hot, as we'd forgotten to switch on the electric fan. Sunshine streamed in golden bars from the window, swathing the bed, motes of dust twirling in the light. I'd forgotten to draw the shutters.

There was rain in the sunshine, of course. It added strange spotty shadows to the spiralling motes. I could hear its thin spatter above us on the galvanized iron roof.

Ding dong.

Oh! The front door.

I shook myself. Wake up, Rosa. Pay attention.

Something with sharp teeth nibbled in the pit of my stomach and in a rush it all came back to me: waiting for Danny on the promenade, Father and the postcard, Danny's appearance in the wee hours of the morning, Father rushing to take Danny to the hospital.

Ding dong.

Oh yes. And the doorbell. I'd had no idea we had a doorbell until a few days ago. And now here it was ding-donging every few minutes.

Ding dong.

I nudged Yaya but she simply pulled more of the

sheet around her and snored on. She could sleep for a hundred years.

I looked at the time on my new mobile.

9:00 a.m.

It must be Father. Yaya had dutifully bolted the front door firmly from the inside as per Father's paranoid instructions. He couldn't let himself in.

I climbed out of bed, my muscles creaking like dried wood. My head was stuffed with wool and my mouth tasted sour. I was exhausted.

I threw off my nightie and pulled on my jeans and T-shirt from the day before. Stumbled down the stairs, my bare feet sliding around on the polished boards.

Frankly I wasn't looking forward to seeing Father again, even if he owed me a massive explanation. Our problems loomed huge and heavy, and I didn't feel like confronting them this morning. But what about Danny?

The thought of Danny made my feet skate more quickly to the front door.

Ding dong.

Lock the door, Father had told Yaya before he left. And she'd done exactly that. Bolting every single barrel of the five Father had installed long ago when

Mother was still alive. Our high-security prison was on red alert.

I couldn't reach the topmost bolt. I hurried to the kitchen to fetch a chair. Dragged it over. Climbed up.

Ding dong.

I could hear Father drumming his fingers impatiently on the other side of the door. Give me a break, Father.

The last bolt gave an almighty screech.

I jumped off the chair and pulled the door open.

In my belly, the sharp teeth clamped down, hard.

Even after all these years, I recognized that sweep of hair, those eyes, that face.

Mother.

26

Would a ghost have eyes like these? Bewildered, dark and deep. And warm, creamed coffee skin, beaded with rain? Would a ghost have long, black hair, slippery wet, blowing about in the sea gusts? Would a ghost's dress cling wetly to her, would she run a tongue over her dry lips, as she stared at me? Would a ghost carry a massive suitcase that made a heavy smacking noise as she dropped it on the floor?

Mother is dead, Father said.

Mother is dead, Yaya said.

They lied.

I'd always imagined that I would throw myself into her arms, cover her face with kisses.

But I didn't. I couldn't move. This must be what it's like to be struck by lightning – burning and frozen at the same time.

My hands moved awkwardly.

Mother?

Her hand flew to cover her mouth. Her eyes flickered all over my face as if she was searching for something.

She made a helpless gesture at me.

'You are her child. Oh my God. She and Jon had a *baby* and I didn't know.'

The voice was low, musical. And I realized as I gazed at her, thunderstruck, that her neck arched perfect and smooth from her shoulders. She couldn't be Mother. She didn't have the Calm.

I watched, fascinated, as a tear appeared on her lashes and quivered there for a long moment before finally trickling down her cheek. She brushed it away and then reached out a hesitant hand.

Her fingers brushed my cheek. 'God. You look just like Kara at that age.'

She laughed a strange coughing laugh and suddenly her eyes were roaming over me hungrily, as if I might vanish and she had to memorize every little detail quickly.

Confusion and fear gnawed inside me. I began to sign, forgetting that she might not be able to understand sign language. *Who are you?*

But the signing didn't faze her. She just nodded

and her hands moved automatically, signing fluently as she spoke.

'My name is Kat.'

Kat!

Not Kara, but Kat.

'I'm sorry. You must be . . . shocked. Your mother . . . Kara and I are' – she closed her eyes, as she corrected herself – 'Kara and I *were* twins. *Identical* twins.'

I could not move or look away. We looked at each other. Looked and looked and looked, our eyes starving, greedy things.

'What is *your* name?'

I hesitated at first then spelled out my name with stiff fingers. *R-O-S-A*.

She smiled. 'Rosa? Oh! When we were little, Kara had a dolly named Rosa. How she loved that doll.'

Then she trembled and I realized with a start that she was soaked through by the rain.

Social graces, Rosa! It was Yaya's voice I imagined bellowing in my ear, even though she was fast asleep in my bed upstairs. *Have you no manners, girl? Were you born in a goat shed?*

I ducked my head and gestured dazedly towards the

living room. *Come in*, I signed. *Would you like some tea?*

'Oh!' Kat smiled and her gaze swept warmly over me. 'Thank you.'

Her eyes lifted. Suddenly she seemed to be seeing everything. And her seeing made me see too, and for the first time I saw my life from someone else's point of view: the whitewashed walls, the crack in the ceiling above the front door, the shabby tiles on the hallway floor, the neat row of green wellies by the door, the steep wooden staircase. It wasn't fancy but it had always felt like home.

So why did I feel that twinge of shame? Why did I want to rush away to the kitchen to fetch the mop and bucket, the better to wipe the floor, make it look a little bit shinier?

It was better when I led her into the living room. There was comfort in its disarray. There was nothing lonely or bare about the sofas and rugs, the picture frames on the side table, the cushions on the chairs. Even the mess of wet towels still piled on the centre table looked comforting.

She reached out, tucking a strand of hair behind my ear, caressing my cheek. 'I can't get over how gorgeous you are.'

My cheeks warmed at the compliment.

She frowned. 'You had no idea Kara had a sister, did you? Jon never told you?'

I shook my head slowly.

'I can't blame them,' She sighed. 'I . . . I wasn't sure if I would be welcome. The other day I . . . I actually rang the doorbell. But . . . I lost my nerve. I couldn't stay. I was afraid.'

She bowed, shamefaced. 'I . . . I hid behind some trees when Jon came out. It was ridiculous of me, I know. But I just wasn't ready.'

She rang the doorbell! It was her! A bitter fire began to smoulder in my chest. Father lied to me. He'd been lying to me since Mother died. He said Mother had no living kin. He said she was an only child. But he lied. Where had Kat been all these years? What had happened between the sisters?

Kat sat down on the sofa.

The floor was strewn with Father's books from last night, the shredded postcard scattered all over the floor like popcorn.

And then realization struck me like a thunderbolt. Father's postcard. It wasn't from Mother. It was from Kat:

Jon

    We'll be together again soon, my darling. I'm coming.
Please don't push me away. Take me back.
    I love you.
    K

27

I walked in on you searching my wardrobe. That was the first time I realized something was wrong.

You were on your knees, ferreting through the pile of shoes and stuff on the cabinet floor, really searching.

What on earth were you looking for? I stood, arms folded across my chest, watching.

What did you want now, Kat? You'd become a total harridan since that incident with your boyfriend. What was *that* all about, eh? Why did you decide to turn my existence into a dirty little secret? Were you afraid I would snatch him away? Did you still feel like the disadvantaged twin, sharing a cot with another baby who grabbed all your toys and pushed you aside so that Mama would feed her first?

I was just about to tap you on the shoulder when you whirled round.

And oh, Kat, the guilt and horror on your face! I'd caught you at something! You turned beet-red with shame, your mouth wide open, your eyes so round the whites showed.

You looked so horrified, so absurd, that I laughed. This was what came of a childhood of competing over who owned what.

Look at you! I signed. I think that at the back of my mind I thought you were just stealing a pair of my socks, like when we were teenagers.

And then the fright ebbed from your face and it was replaced by something else. An expression I didn't recognize. Crafty, sly.

You held something up in one hand.

It was a scarf I'd bought in Camden Market, during those early days of touristic trawling.

'This is his,' you said. And you could barely mask the triumph in your voice. *Caught you!* your eyes accused. *Guilty!*

And, of course, I immediately *felt* guilty. Immediately thought I must have done something wrong, frantically searching my mind for a way to explain why I had wronged you, why I had done *it*.

But what was '*it*'? *This is HIS*, you'd said. WHOSE?

The funny thing was: I didn't connect it with Jon at all. I hadn't seen him since you went out on that date. You had not mentioned him to me and I had not dared ask how it went. You were in such a mood afterwards, huffing and puffing, I told myself to leave it, that we would look back on this when we were old and would both laugh it off.

No, Jon never crossed my mind.

It's mine, I signed, nonchalant.

And just like that you exploded.

'You WITCH, Kara! How can you do this to me! Why are you seeing Jon in secret? Why are you so OBSESSED with him?'

It was like a legion of demons had taken residence in your heart, contaminated your brain with awful thoughts, filled you with venom. You were taken over.

I tried to respond to the accusations you spat at me like sharp stones. But I couldn't sign fast enough.

'How dare you? How dare you try to steal my fiancé?'

Fiancé? I signed. *You didn't tell me you were engaged.*

'Not yet. But we will be. I love him and he loves me. But you're trying to come between us.'

Stop! Stop! I signed. *Have you gone mad? I haven't seen him since!*

But you were not to be stopped. 'You can't have him, Kara. You can't take everything away from me. You took our parents' love. Now you are taking Jon's.'

Took our parents' love? What are you talking about? Don't be STUPID! I signed. And it *was* stupid. Such a stupid situation. In fact, it was so ridiculous that I began to laugh hysterically.

And you stared at me, disbelieving. I can recognize that look in your eyes now, know hatred when I see it. But I didn't, then. I didn't understand how far into the abyss you'd fallen. Until you drew back your arm.

I wasn't prepared for it. I just stood there, an easy target. When your hand connected with my cheek it made a sharp sound, like a gunshot.

The sudden pain brought tears to my eyes. I know I should have been angry. But it was fear that surged inside me. Fear that must have shone in my eyes as I stood there, one hand cooling my scorched cheek.

You stared at your hand as if it was something totally independent of you. As if it had attacked of its own accord.

And then your eyes flickered to mine and I saw realization dawn. I saw you blink yourself awake as if you were emerging from a bad dream.

'Oh, Kara!' you cried. 'Oh!' And then you threw your arms round me, inconsolable. Weeping. 'I don't know what came over me.' You said it over and over. 'That wasn't me, Kara, I promise!'

I held you, bewildered. Held you tight. And then later as you apologized over and over again, I signed in soft soothing shapes, *It's all right, it's all right.*

But it was never all right. Never again. The monster didn't go away. It bided its time inside you. Waiting. Growing in strength. And slowly it took over. Replacing the blood that ran in your veins with something rancid, bitter. Replacing your soft heart with something twisted and sour.

You watched me. You tried to hide it, but I knew. The slyness was unmistakeable. It was like you'd donned a plastic mask: hard, smiling, immobile, fake. You, but not you.

And you continued to look through my stuff, search my wardrobe, rifle through my room. Searching, searching for evidence of betrayal. You were so obvious. I could see where you'd been in the untidiness of clothing refolded, notebooks left open on the wrong page, drawers left ajar.

Then you began to turn up at the flat at random times, checking up on me. When I asked you why you weren't at work, you said you were having a little break. But how many little breaks could a nurse have? How were you managing to leave the hospital so often at so many odd times of the day?

Jon suddenly featured in every conversation. But it was always so perverse, Kat! You managed to turn the most ordinary things into an accusation.

'How do you like that new coffee I bought?' you might ask.

Delicious, I would signal.

'Did Jon think it was great too?'

And I could only stare at you and wonder.

It made me angry. What unreasonable game were you playing? Were you paying me back for silly jealousies when we were little? Well, I thought, it was preposterous.

We rowed over it, shouted at each other. You were accusing, unbelieving, horrible.

And always after a spell of confrontation, you backed down,

abject remorse making your body shudder. 'What's wrong with me, Kara? I can't help my jealousy, I just can't help it.'

And I forgave you every time. Of course I did. You and me, Kat, we are sisters. I had no choice but to forgive you because leaving was not an option, was it?

We are family. We are for ever.

Besides, this petty craziness was going to go away. I was sure of it.

Jon was concerned, Kat.

One moment, you were his gorgeous date, excited to be with him, the next . . . you were accusing him of betrayal. Faced with this weirdness, he didn't have to hang around. Any ordinary guy would probably have walked away. But he didn't.

That's why he came to see me. He waited until he knew you would be at work, knocked on our door. When I opened it, I was shocked.

The man who stood on our threshold was not the swash-buckling stranger who kissed me by mistake. His hair fell long over his eyes, eyes that peered at me full of sorries and regret before he'd even begun to explain what he was doing there.

And silly me, my instinct was to slam the door in his face. What was he doing here? He caused all this trouble. It was all *his* fault!

He must have known I might shut the door. Because as I

swung it shut, he pushed a foot in the crack and I found myself staring at his anguished face through that narrow corridor. I pushed back, trying to force the door shut. He winced but he didn't remove his foot.

'Look, let me in. We have to talk about Kat. Just . . . just tell me. Tell me how I can fix it,' he said, his voice tired, his eyes pale like water. Worn out. And I realized: this was the face of a good man. He didn't have to be here, but here he was. He had you in his heart, Kat.

And I also realized that I couldn't do it alone. I couldn't fix you all by myself. I needed help.

So I let him in.

And that's how it began, Kat.

It began with you and it was always about you. Jon and I were just trying to figure you out. We wanted to make YOU happy. You were our project, can you see that? Will you ever understand?

We had to meet secretly to discuss you, to try to find a solution.

And then we found ourselves meeting for no reason other than to see each other again.

Whenever our secret coffees and lunches and meetings in the park came to an end, it was always agony to part.

Suddenly I had insight into your delusion, Kat. Because, like you, I couldn't get Jon out of my mind. When I was with him, I couldn't take my eyes off him.

We never meant it to happen. Never. We'd been through months of anxiety and frustration over you . . . and suddenly we found ourselves smiling again, laughing together, happy. It was good. But what a calamity. How could something so good be so bad? Well.

And there you were, continuing to make your mad accusations, continuing to attack, continuing to suspect us. And all the while, Jon and I were making your delusions come true.

28

*Y*ou sent Father a postcard.

It was all I could do to keep my hands from shaking as I signed.

She tilted her head to one side, a quizzical expression on her face.

Father was reading a postcard last night, I signed. *It was from you.*

'What postcard?'

I gestured to the torn-up bits on the table.

She stared at the mess, her face uncomprehending. And then slowly she reached for a small strip, picked it up, stared at the bright red of the London bus. Turned it over to reveal a fragment of long, slanted handwriting.

'It's . . . it's all torn up.'

At first her face was blank. And then understanding dawned in her eyes. Her face contorted. Her brows drew together, her mouth twisted.

Suddenly she threw her head back and howled

a shrill howl. Desperate, hurt, furious. Inhuman.

I recoiled, frightened.

Her eyes lifted up to mine and her pupils dilated. It was as if she was seeing me for the first time. 'You! *What are* you *doing here?*' She rose, her fists clenched.

I backed away from her, my throat emitting terrified noises. '*Ungh ungh ungh!*'

'KARA!' she cried, lunging forward, her hands clawing for my neck.

Kara? Did she suddenly think I was Mother? I shook my head, throwing myself out the living-room door and scrambling towards the stairs. What was wrong? What had happened? Oh, Yaya, wake up, Yaya. Help! My twisted throat shrilled dumbly, '*AAAAAAH! AAAAAAH!*'

I managed to leap up to the first landing but a hand closed round my ankle. I pitched forward, my head cracking against the banister.

'KARA!' she screamed as she tried to drag me down the stairs, her fingers like steel claws. 'KARA!' Her face pushed up close to mine. 'How *dare* you, Kara?' she hissed. 'How dare you take Jon from me?'

I tried to push her off, to pry her claws off me, but she had me pinioned firmly to the stairs.

And then her hands were round my neck,

squeezing. Tears were shining on her cheeks. 'I want you *gone*! I want you out of my life, you *monster*!'

I stared at her as she throttled me, those eyes bulging with fury, the whites showing, teeth bared, deep lines creasing the sides of her face, hair wild, veins bulging in her neck. Her fingers were vice-like, unbudgeable, relentlessly squeezing the life out of me.

They say you see your life flashing before your eyes when you die. Well, as life began to leave, that didn't really happen. Instead, time went into slow mo, my mind calmly observing and thinking as it watched my body slowly fading away.

And all I could think was: God's made a mistake. This is a terrible design fault. Why do we only breathe through nose and mouth? So easily choked off. Why couldn't other parts of the body take in air? Why not the fingertips? Why not the knees?

No air. No air.

I stared up at that face. Mother's eyes. Mother's lips. Mother's hair. But no, not Mother. Why did Kat want to murder me?

My vision began to darken. It was like the sun had a dimmer and someone had turned it down low. Mood lighting. Thin glimmers of light spidered around my killer's face. Perhaps I was dreaming. Perhaps I was going to wake up to find that none of this had ever happened, no beach, no postcard, no Danny, no monster killing me on the stairs?

I tried to gasp, tried to suck in some air, but only a tired little *akk!* came out of my throat.

Then a weird tingling sensation began to ripple through my body. This was it. The end. What was it going to be like on the other side? Would there be choirs of heavenly angels and gilded, curlicued gates to Heaven with wise Saint Peter nodding wisely at the door in a white nightie? Or was all that religion totally wrong? Was I just going to go *pffft* like a blown-out flame?

I couldn't move, couldn't stir. My muscles had turned into lifeless rubber. I wanted to close my eyes . . . sleep. But something in me struggled. Something in me still wanted to fight.

The face above me was wavering and zigzagging like a bad picture on the television. My vision was doubling.

Except. Over my murderer's angry grimace was the face of another.

OK, this must be the final hallucination. The other face was a thin gauzy sheen superimposed on my attacker's. The other face was smiling, the eyes gentle, loving.

My heart leaped. *Mother, is that you?*

The lips smiled and moved. *Ro-sa.*

Have you come to take me? Take me now, Mother!

She shook her head. *Ro-sa.*

Wild joy exploded in my chest, hot and spreading. The last laugh was on Father. There *were* such things as ghosts. And won't Yaya be pleased. She wasn't being so ridiculous after all, insisting on me shoving salt into my pocket.

Salt. In my pocket.

Mother nodded.

I willed energy into the dying muscles of my arm. Pushed my hand into my pocket. There it was, the stupid salt. That grainy stuff rubbing awkwardly inside my pocket since Yaya freaked out over the knock on the door. I closed my fist over it.

And swung it into the eyes of my attacker.

Kat screamed.

And then the world blew itself out.

29

Being dead was a bit like drowning in thick syrup. I struggled, swimming slowly up until my head broke the cold, sticky surface, my mouth opening, the air slowly re-inflating my lungs.

My eyes focused slowly and, oh! Mother, you were there, looking down at me, your hair falling over one eye. You smiled and I smiled back.

Mother— I began . . .

You leaned up close and slowly, and you became real. I could feel the solid pillow of your cheek against mine, the flutter of your lashes on my forehead, the cool trace of your fingertips on my face. This was Heaven then, just me and you. And I was glad. Oh, so glad.

'No, no, no, no . . .'

I started. Sat up. No, not Heaven.

I was on the sofa in the living room. The shutters were shut over the window, but light seeped in along the frame like some kind of holy glow.

Slowly I became aware of myself again. My muscles were soft fatty lumps of jelly, sending crackles of pain all over my body. My throat. Oh, it was so sore! The air moving through my airways had sharp fingernails that caught in the raw red walls.

I smelled the thick noxious odour of cigarette smoke and instinct leaped inside me. Smoking inside the house! Yaya will go berserk!

But Yaya was nowhere to be seen.

It was Kat, of course, smoking in the far corner.

Staring at her, it still took my breath away. What was the word for it? Dopo something . . . no. Doppelgänger. That's it.

She was Mother's doppelgänger.

But there was nothing hilarious about this. Doppelgänger Week seemed a million years ago.

The suitcase she had dropped in the doorway was now in the middle of the living-room floor. Between us, like a barrier. She stood against the wall, hair over her face, one shoulder exposed by a long tear in the sleeve of her blouse while one restless hand cradled an elbow gently. Her bare feet worked the floor, shuffling, edgy. She pressed against the wall, pressed and pressed as if she wanted to push herself right into the plaster, push herself away into nothingness.

She sucked nervously on the cigarette stub and I wrinkled my nose at the awful curling stink. I imagined all that smoke filling her lungs, her heart, her arteries, her brain. Fouling everything inside her. Filling her with evil.

She tossed her head, pushed the sheet of straggly hair away from her eyes and I realized that she'd been watching me under all that hair. She was whispering to herself. 'I didn't, didn't, didn't do it. It wasn't me. I wouldn't! I wouldn't!'

There was something cold on my neck. I touched it. A damp, folded towel. I pressed the skin under the towel and my vision blurred with pain. This was where she'd had me in a death grip.

There was something on my forehead. I raised a leaden arm. It was a bandage. The first-aid pouch that Father had installed in the bathroom was lying unzipped on the table, plasters, ointments, tape and tablets spilt everywhere.

She must have carried me to the sitting room when I passed out. Cooled the injuries on my neck with a wet towel. Found the first-aid kit. Cleaned up the cut on my forehead. Stuck a bandage on it.

But why would she do that? Why would she hurt me and then fix me up?

She was rubbing her face with one hand now, rubbing, rubbing, rubbing, as if she wanted to erase her face.

I was afraid to look away. What if she went crazy again? I managed a glance at the door. Could I make a run for it? Oh! The baseball bat! . . . But I got rid of it, didn't I? Now I had nothing to defend myself with and it was my own fault.

She looked at me and smiled. I was taken aback. It was such a natural smile, a *normal* smile.

'Lovely,' she whispered. 'You're lovely, Rosa.'

Kat said it with such feeling, it made me feel strange: drawn to her and repelled at the same time.

She straightened her back, took a step forward. For a moment, I had the oddest feeling that she was going to run across the room and take me into her arms.

But she didn't. She turned to the wall, huddling against it, the smoke from her cigarette wrapping around her in a white shroud.

'Will you ever forgive me?' She shook her head slowly and great big tears fell from her eyes. She sank down to her haunches, back still pressed against the wall.

Her eyes watched me across the room.

'The last time I saw Kara, it was a strange day.

The rain actually stopped. Imagine that! Who would have thought the rain would actually *stop* in Mirasol?'

She leaned her head on the wall.

'That was years ago. I'd come over to Mirasol from London. That's where I'd been living – where I've lived all this time. It was a short holiday, and I just wanted to see if it had changed, just wanted to be home again.'

She laughed.

'Oh, it hadn't changed at all! Rain when my plane landed, rain all the way to the hotel, rain when I visited the market near our old home. And I thought, If there's anything you could count on in Mirasol, it was the weather! And just as the thought popped into my head, the rain stopped.'

She bowed her head.

'I wandered around the market for a while, looking at all the familiar things. Smelling all the familiar smells. It was great to be home. And then suddenly Kara just appeared out of nowhere. I jumped out of my skin. Thought I was seeing a phantom. Thought I'd gone out of my mind. I hadn't seen her for . . . what, six years?

She drew deeply from the cigarette, then stubbed

it out on the wooden floorboard. Yaya would have been apoplectic. But this was not the time to worry about what Yaya thought.

'But it *was* her. Kara hurried up to me as if nothing had ever happened between us. She threw her arms around me and we were so full of joy at seeing each other again that we wept shamelessly.'

The day the sun shone.

The day Mother died.

There I was, remembering, five years old again, standing in the bright sunshine, staring at all the new things, full of wonder and maybe a little bit afraid to be out in the world. And then there I was waving bye-bye as Mother bade me wait by the baskets. *Back soon*, Mother had signed.

Kat's hands moved nervously over her eyes, flicking at her hair. 'We hung onto each other like we would never let go. We were in heaven! Together again!' Her eyes pleaded with me. 'Please understand, it was the happiest moment in my life. We'd been apart for so long and I missed Kara so much. I *love* Kara, you understand? I love her.'

I stared at the woman, wondering. She was Mother's *identical* twin. They looked alike, were grown in the same womb, shared the same DNA, the same genes, the same building blocks.

Which meant I shared her DNA too. I shivered. We could be mother and daughter.

'Kara started to say something,' Kat continued. 'She said, "Oh my God, Kat, I have a—" But she never finished the sentence. She just smiled and hugged me again. I realize now she was about to say, "I have a daughter." But she decided not to.' Her mouth twisted. 'And then Kara was chattering away – her hands were everywhere, fluttering like butterflies, telling me that Jon had a job in the hospital and Jon had found a house and Jon . . .' She grimaced. 'Jon. Jon. Jon. Jon. Jon. She wanted to tell me about her life, about how things were OK.'

She closed her eyes.

'That was when it happened.'

She clasped her hands together like she was begging me for something.

'I . . . I just couldn't – *can't* – stop it. It's always there. It lives inside me whether I like it or not. It . . . it just takes over and I can't . . . I can't . . .' She shook her head. 'The demon just came, it . . . it wanted to destroy her. Lashed out at her.'

Demon? Suddenly despite the heat, the noxious clouds of cigarette smoke hanging in the still air, despite the closeness of the shuttered room, I felt cold.

She turned her tortured face to the wall.

'Suddenly we were struggling. I ripped the scarf from her neck. Screamed to the world. Look! Look! The Calm!'

She whirled towards me, her eyes begging. 'But it was the demon! It wanted to show the world what she really was. It wanted her destroyed.'

The demon. She was talking as if her will was not her own. As if she was not one person but two.

'The market went *wild*.' Kat's voice echoed in the living room. 'It was like . . . like those horror movies when a village takes up pitchforks and sets off to destroy the ogre. They were insatiable, chased her like an animal, hunted her. She ran – and for a while I was part of the hunt, snapping at her heels like the rest of them, howling for her blood. But then I woke up. Heard the screams coming from my throat. I was shocked. Fell back. Hid in a clump of bamboo by the side of the road. But nobody noticed, of course. They could only see *her*.'

I realized that I'd been holding my breath. I made myself take in air, my chest rising and falling.

'What they would have done if they'd caught her I

never found out. Because suddenly she ran onto the road . . . and then there was a small bus, coming too fast round the corner. And . . .'

Kat shook her head, her face ruined.

'She was my life, you understand? I loved her more than anything. And yet there was this . . . this *thing* inside me that just wouldn't leave her alone. Just wouldn't stop until . . .'

She buried her face in her knees for a long moment. When she lifted her face up again, a light from the window fell like a spotlight on her face.

'She lay there, the life spilling out of her onto the road. Her eyes searching everywhere.' Her voice dropped to a whisper. 'I thought she was looking for me. I was ashamed. So ashamed. I hid from her eyes. But she wasn't looking for me, was she? She was looking for you!'

Kat's chin dropped to her chest and her body collapsed, gaunt and listless against the wall.

I found myself on my feet, unsteadily making my way towards her.

She cried out, cowering. 'Don't. Don't come any closer.'

But then her face became alert, her head tilted to one side, listening. There was the sound of keys in the front door and the creak of hinges opening.

Father called from the hall, 'Yaya! I thought I told you to bolt the door!'

And I saw it. Saw the shivering, cowering, beaten creature huddled across the room suddenly vanish.

And in its place came the thing she feared. She became someone else, eyes big with anticipation, lips parted, rosy and expectant, shoulders thrown back, chin high, skin suddenly glowing.

Ecstatic.

'Jon!' she cried. 'Jon! At last!'

30

I 've always wondered, Kat, what would have happened if on that first evening you'd managed to laugh off the mistaken kiss, if you'd simply gone out and had a lovely first date with Jon and nothing but gladness in your heart.

Would it have been you married to Jon years later, a gorgeous baby in your arms? If your morbid delusions had not changed you so, would it have been you and Jon, holding hands and planning your happily ever after?

Would it have been you, guilty about the sister you exchanged for a lifetime of happy families? Guilty about the sister you left behind?

But there's no point wondering about any of it. You were on a path, Kat, and somehow you lost your way. And I was on that path too. But somehow I found myself with Jon.

Love is strange. It's an acute kind of loneliness, isn't it? That constant yearning for the other person. That hunger. I didn't think it was possible but there it was. It's not pleasure but pain.

I saw it in your face, felt it in my gut. You loved Jon, but Jon loved me. And as for me? Why, I loved you both. It was a vicious circle. We were all hurting, obsessed.

Jon and I ducked and weaved. Met in secret places. And you searched and spied. And when you accused us, we lied. We denied everything.

At the beginning we were wrongly accused, but by the end we were guilty, guilty, guilty.

I'm so sorry, Kat. So sorry.

I promise you, Kat, it tormented us as much as it did you. It almost drove us apart.

I was all for telling you everything, for revealing the truth about Jon and me. I told Jon: it will shake her awake! Bring her to her senses! I think I believed that telling you would somehow wrongfoot the madness.

But Jon disagreed. I'm a doctor and I should know, he argued. It's a mental illness and Kat has no idea. No insight into what's wrong.

Psychiatrists called it delusional disorder. An unreasonable paranoia. An unshakeable belief in something that does not exist. People with delusional disorder could function normally – except when it came to the object of their delusion.

Delusional disorder was highly uncommon, the doctors told us. Rare! There are treatments, but sufferers don't often seek help. How can you seek help if you don't know, don't want to know, that you are ill?

They wanted to meet you, find out more, study you like a

germ under a microscope. *Rare*, they said, licking their lips like it was some wonderful, delicious thing.

One doctor told us: All you can do is humour her. Try not to upset her.

Another doctor said: She can live a good life, a fruitful life, if you remove the source of the obsession.

How impossible was that?

Your delusions. Our love. It was a catastrophe.

That final afternoon, Jon and I returned to the flat after lunch knowing that you would be at work. It was winter, and though it was mid-afternoon, it was dark. The flat was all shadows.

It was only when we switched on the light that we realized you were sitting in a chair in the living room.

Open on your lap was a book I'd bought on delusional disorder, the pages yellow with all my desperate highlighting.

Jon and I drew back, afraid. But you didn't seem to see Jon. Your eyes pegged themselves on me. Eyes that begged me to say it wasn't true.

'Is this what you think, Kara? You think I'm delusional?'

I couldn't speak. If I said no, I would be lying. If I said yes, it would be like handing you a life sentence. Certifying you insane. Whatever I chose to do or say would be the end of everything.

So I just stood there, frozen to the spot.

Then Jon stepped forward, clearing his throat. 'Kat,' he said softly. 'We think it's time you saw a doctor.'

It was a mistake. Jon should have known better.

I saw your eyes go from mine to Jon's. I saw the terrible realization dawn on your face. It wasn't the crazy suspicion that had transformed you since this thing began, but a genuine realization of betrayal. A look of hurt. That was when I watched your world fall apart, Kat. Heard your heart splinter into a million pieces.

Then that horrid, swarming thing engulfed you again, pushing your warm, living soul out of your poor body.

You used the book. It was thick, jacketed in a hard cover with sharp corners. We were so dumbstruck by the moment, and you moved so quickly that when you started hitting me with it I didn't move away and Jon just watched. You struck quickly and suddenly. With all your might. In the face. On my head. Over and over and over. I heard Jon's shouts as huge chunks of darkness fell around me. Everything went black, black, black. I saw tiny stars in the blackness. Jon grappled with you but you were unstoppable. Still managing to land hits as I lay prostrate and dazed. Your strength was inhuman, that vengeful spirit, relentless.

I don't think I would have survived if Jon had not been there. You wanted me dead.

But Jon managed to wrestle the book from you and hold you down, pinning your flailing wrists to the carpet.

I shook my head, shook the darkness off. I saw you looking up at him, begging him to look at you and only at you.

'Oh, Jon,' you cried. 'You love me, don't you? You love *me*! Tell her that! Make her stop trying to take you away!'

Jon shook his head. 'I don't love you, Kat.'

'Don't say that, Jon, you don't mean it! *You love me!*' And you pulled your wrists from him, threw your arms round him. Tried to take him in an embrace.

Jon recoiled. 'Kat, listen to me,' he shouted. 'I. DON'T. LOVE. YOU.'

'Yes you do!' And you arched shamelessly under him. 'You do love me, Jon!'

Jon pushed you away. 'I'm so sorry, Kat. I don't. It's Kara I love. I love Kara.'

And I steeled myself, waiting for that vindictive monster to return, waiting for that poisonous curtain to crash down again.

But it didn't come. You suddenly fell back, lying limp on the carpet, your eyes closed. And Jon slowly sat back on his heels.

'Oh my God,' you whispered. And your eyes flew open, searching his and then flickering to me, staring at the blood trickling down my face as if you'd only just noticed it for the first time.

And you looked so devastated I knelt down, wanting to take your hand, wanting to reassure you. I love Jon, but I love you too, Kat. I will always be there for you.

But you began to struggle once more and at first I thought

the fight was going to start up all over again. But you were pushing Jon away, suddenly screaming as if you were afraid.

'Get away from me! Get away!' You turned to Jon. 'Take her away, please. Leave me.'

Jon got to his feet. At first I thought he was just going to see to my injuries, but instead he put his arms round me, lifted me bodily and began to manhandle me towards the door.

What did he think he was doing? Couldn't he see that Kat needed help? I wriggled in his arms, banged on his chest with my fists. We needed to stay, we needed to help you. How were you going to cope? How could we leave you like this?

My twisted throat shrilled hideously as the door shut behind us. '*Ungh ungh ungh!*'

Jon dragged me out onto the street, hailed a cab and pushed me in.

I screamed and scrabbled for the door handle, tried to get out again. But Jon held me back, shouting at the driver to take us to the nearest Emergency department.

'It's all for the best,' he whispered, putting his arms round me in a tight embrace. 'We have to leave her, Kara.'

Jon and I wrote letters, sent you the names of doctors. But you never replied. Never returned Jon's phone calls. You packed all my things and had them delivered to Jon's flat. And then you packed yourself up, moved somewhere else. Moved jobs.

She can live a good life, a fruitful life, if you remove the source of the obsession, the doctor had told us. So you removed yourself from us. Disappeared from our lives.

And that was how you gave me a chance for happiness. You did it for me, didn't you, Kat? You knew I would never want us separated.

You knew that parting company was the only way you could save me from you.

31

As Father walked into the room, Kat unfolded from where she had cowered against the wall.

She was like a cat, slinky and purring and long, putting each paw delicately in front of the other, almond eyes wide with enticing.

'Jon, at *last*.' And the way she said it, so musically, the vowels so round, the consonants so crisp, I had a sudden vision of her, lonely, in front of a mirror, practising a thousand times for just this moment.

Relief surged in my chest. Father could fix this. He could sort this out. Figure out what was going on. Banish this scary spectre. Put his big warm arms round me and make it all go away.

But Father just stood there. He was frozen to the floorboards in the doorway. Like that woman who turned into a pillar of salt in one of Yaya's favourite Bible stories. He looked useless with fear.

'Did you get my postcards?' she asked, her face eager.

She had written more than one? I stared at Father. Did he know she was coming? The other night, when the doorbell rang, he'd run out into the darkness crying, *Is it you?* He must have thought she'd come knocking. And all that security fuss, bolting the bolts and installing the CCTV.

He didn't move. Didn't speak. Father was pale at the best of times, but now all the colour had drained from his skin. His blue eyes were cold marbles sunk deep in his white face.

'I knew you were here in Mirasol,' Kat said. 'I knew . . . but I was a mess. I wanted to forget about you. Forget about Kara. Forget about everything. And then I saw that article in the *Medical Journal*.'

Her eyes flashed and her voice subsided to a purr. 'It was a lovely piece about all your brilliant work on the island. About how you helped your patients overcome stigma and superstition to live full lives.'

She tossed her hair. 'Mirasol! Not the easiest place for a doctor of the Calm to work in. Not a place where someone with the Calm would choose to live. After reading it, I felt like I'd just woken up from a long, dreamless sleep. Oh, Jon, I could feel again, my blood flowed warm and alive for the first time in years. And I knew what I had to do. I needed to be with you.'

Father's lips set to a thin line and the blue marbles were hard, expressionless.

But Kat seemed oblivious. 'It wasn't that hard to find you. There's always someone who knows someone who knows someone who knows something.' She gestured silkily towards the suitcase. 'I couldn't help myself. I just had to come and see how you were. Oh, Jon.'

Coyly she reached out. Touched him on the chest.

It was as if someone had stuck a pin into him, as if he had been shaken awake. He swung towards me. 'Rosa! What did she do to you, sweetheart?'

I stumbled across the floor, met him halfway. Oh, the bliss of Father's arms around me. I felt safe at last.

Kat screamed. 'Sweetheart? *Sweetheart!?*' She grabbed my shoulders and tried to rip me from Father's arms. 'You *witch*, Kara!'

I shrank from her.

But Kat wasn't even looking at me. She shouldered me aside, grabbing Father's shirt. 'How could you, Jon? How could you betray me with my own *sister*?'

'Sister?' Father's face crumpled. 'Kat, Kara is dead. Long ago dead.'

With a scream, she snatched me up, her fingers painful on my arms. She shook me violently. '*You!* Always getting in the way! Why do you do this to me, Kara?'

'STOP IT!' Father pushed himself between us, grabbing Kat's wrists and twisting so that she let go of me with a sharp cry. 'Enough, Kat! This is not Kara. This is Rosa, my daughter.'

Kat's eyes blazed angrily toward me. She folded her arms across her chest and laughed. '*Daughter?* You can be so cruel, darling. Do you think I don't recognize my own twin sister?'

But Father ignored her, his arm round me, urging me towards the door. 'Rosa, let's get out of here.'

Kat threw herself at him, frantic. But at her touch, Father recoiled, shuddering as if it was not a woman but a rotting corpse that had touched him.

She tried to pull him close. 'Oh, Jon, you silly billy.'

But Father's face contorted, his mouth a grimace. He spoke in a low guttural growl. 'There is no Kara. Kara is gone and you should know.' His hands were suddenly on her shoulders. 'You killed her, Kat.'

Kat slapped his hands off and stumbled away, a bewildered look on her face.

'Killed?' Her voice was high, hysterical. 'But here she is! What are you talking about?'

'*KARA IS DEAD!*' It was an animal roar. 'She's dead because of *you!*'

Kat clapped her hands over her heart. 'You're lying,' she gasped. 'Why are you saying that to me? Why would I kill my own sister?'

But Father didn't reply. Instead, he lowered his head, planted his hands on her shoulders and pushed her away. He was so strong she tumbled across the room, a tiny leaf flicked away by a typhoon wind.

She lay dazed on the floor and Father advanced with his hands closed into hard fists.

'*Ungh ungh ungh,*' I cried, suddenly afraid. But he ignored me.

Kat smiled up at him. 'Darling!' She began to push herself up to her feet but Father grabbed her by the shoulders and threw her down again.

I tugged Father's arm, willing him to look at me. *Stop, Father.*

But he shook me off and grabbed her by the throat.

'I . . . love . . . you,' she gasped.

I began to prise his hands off her neck but his fingers were claws of steel, immovable. He was going to kill her.

Oh, Father, Father, don't do this! I threw my arms round him, pressed my face against his. 'UNGH UNGH UNGH!' It hurt my ravaged throat to call but it worked – Father startled and let go. Kat crumpled, coughing, to the ground.

He looked at me with dazed eyes.

Don't. Please, Father. My signing was rigid with fear.

When he spoke, the breath came out in gulps, like a small child after a big cry. 'She *deserves* it. She's a MONSTER!'

She is NOT a monster. My hands dragged the words out of the air. *She's ILL.*

Not a monster. Wasn't that what Father was always trying to tell me? Don't pay any mind to those horror stories, Rosa. *You are not a monster, you are ill.*

It was enough.

With a choked cry Father knelt, covering his eyes with his hands.

And over his shoulder, on Kat's face, I saw the waking realization . . . the insight dawning. The horror.

'Oh no, not again,' she whispered to herself. She covered her eyes with her hands. 'Oh, Kara.'

She got unsteadily to her feet and ran out of the room, into the hall. We heard her struggling to open the front door. Heard the creak of its hinges as it swung open, the sudden hiss of outside noise, of rain and wind and whispering sea.

'KARA!' she screamed.

And then the door slammed shut.

32

I ran past Father into the hall.

The front door was ajar, the outside world glowing through the wavering fissure like something mystical.

I pushed it open and stepped out onto the street, shiny and puddling from the morning's rain.

The other houses huddled together at the end of the road like three old women whispering cattily amongst themselves, shutters pointing back at us like fingers, the windows rolling their eyes as if to say, look, some kind of drama is going on over there – twin sisters in love with the same man, imagine, and that one sister, oh, she's out of her head, dangerous, a monster!

'Rosa!' Father cried from inside. 'Come back here!'

But I ignored him, hurrying down the street, peering behind the clumps of bamboo along the curb. I wasn't afraid of Kat any more.

She was Mother's sister. Mother's blood ran

warm in her veins.

Where had she gone? I ran to the end where the other houses sat. There was no sign of anyone on the junction. No sign of anybody on the road scrolling up the mountain.

The beach! I whirled and ran back down the street, skirting our house to follow the sandy path to the promenade, ignoring Father's muffled calls from inside the house. 'Rosa, what are you doing out there? Come back!'

I couldn't turn back. I needed to catch Kat up, grab her by the shoulder, spin her round, make her look at me.

I heard scuffling noises behind me. Feet pounding the sand. Father was close behind.

'Rosa!' he cried. 'Leave her be! I've called the police.'

The police!

I was on the promenade now; the wind stung of salt. I squinted, shielding my eyes with one hand from the white brightness of the sun directly overhead. The water was a cobalt blue, a linen cloth spread flat on the table of ocean.

'Rosa!'

But I just stood and looked. The fringe of slender

coconut trees nodded sleepily over their own shadows and in the long distance, the town was almost a mirage, sunlit through the gauzy screen of rain. I could see no footprints in the sand, no tell-tale trail, no clues to a mad woman's flight.

Disappointment filled my head with a dark chaos. '*Ungh ungh ungh!*' my cries grated into the silence. Where had she gone?

Was she suddenly going to emerge from behind that sand dune? Was she going to step out from behind those coconut trees? She didn't, of course. She had somehow managed to disappear, make herself invisible, the way she'd been invisible all my life.

I heard Father rustling behind me, felt his hand on my shoulder, gentle and warm.

'Let's go, sweetheart. We'll leave her to the police. I've called an ambulance too.'

As if on cue, the wail of sirens rose plaintively in the distance.

Ambulance? I signed. *For what?*

Father patted my shoulder. 'For you, sweetheart.'

When we got to the house, we could hear siren sounds bouncing off the mountain. And Father was suddenly clumsy, fumbling with the keys. When I tried to help, I was even clumsier still, dropping the keys several times before I managed to unlock the door.

And then it didn't matter anyway because the door flew open.

Yaya glared balefully at us in her pink terry bathrobe, hair standing on end, and cheek pleated by pillow marks. 'For God's sake, how is anyone supposed to sleep with the racket you're making?'

33

I felt perfectly fine but the doctors said I had to stay in hospital overnight for observation.

It was strange to be out of my tower. How many times had I fantasized about being somewhere else? How mind-blowing it would be, how exciting! But it wasn't any of those things.

At first it felt odd suddenly being in the company of so many people. I felt itchy and surrounded. Like I was sitting in a nest of swarming ants. But that feeling didn't last very long because in the end, the most mind-blowing thing about the experience was how quickly I got used to it. It was as if I'd spent all my life sitting up in a hospital bed, eating bland food from a tray and ordering tea from a man pushing a trolley in the hall.

It was a noisy room. I could hear the people next door, the soft footsteps of the orderlies and the squeak of the tea trolley. One of the nurses explained it was something to do with the acoustics bouncing sound from everywhere.

So when Father asked Yaya to go home and wait there, in case Kat decided to return, I heard every word of their whispered conversation in the hall.

'If she's acting strange, just humour her, Yaya,' Father whispered. 'You know what humour means?'

'Of course I know how to humour. I humour you all the time, don't I?' Yaya snapped. 'But is she dangerous?'

'Only if you *don't* humour her,' Father snapped back. There was a pause, and when he resumed talking I could hear the effort he was making to sound calm. 'But if she turns up, don't waste any time. Make an excuse, go to the kitchen and phone me, yes?'

Yaya made a huffing noise and left.

But Kat never did return. It was as if she'd waved a magic wand and made herself disappear into thin air.

When the police arrived, their energy had been cinematic. In an instant they were everywhere, prowling about. Yaya hurriedly wrapped a scarf round my neck and stood close, like a super vigilant guard dog.

But the police ignored me as they jogged up and down our road and examined the trees and bushes.

They found nothing. No sign of Kat in the village.

No sign of her on the beach.

They could barely contain their glee when they forced open Kat's suitcase and discovered it was full of gifts for Father, carefully wrapped in glistening paper with beautifully penned dedications. Men's cologne, an expensive leather belt, shirts, a jumper made of Merino wool, a shiny wristwatch. There was no passport, no wallet, no credit cards, no plane ticket. No personal items like clothes and toiletries. No clue of what she was planning to do.

Then the emergency people arrived, brisk, efficient. They made little comment about the Calm.

As they were bundling me into the back of the ambulance, I heard Father explaining to the chief investigating officer that Kat was his dead wife's sister.

'Oh,' the officer said, looking instantly sour and disappointed. 'A domestic disturbance. Ah well. We get a lot of those.'

Later, at the hospital, Father told me that was the precise moment when the police lost interest in investigating the case. All their energy suddenly dissipated and barely minutes after my ambulance departed with Yaya riding shotgun, the police simply packed up, turned off all the blinking lights on their vehicles and drove away.

* * *

After Yaya left for home, Father came back into the room looking exhausted. He sat on the chair next to my bed, his head thrown back.

'Sorry about this, darling,' he said. 'They just want to be sure you're all right, I suppose. I'm certain they'll send you home tomorrow. You look perfectly fine to me.'

It's OK, I signed.

'Good girl.' He sighed and closed his eyes. He looked wan, lying back like that. There were deep lines etched into the corners of his mouth that I swear weren't there before. A deep snore escaped from his lips and he startled awake.

'Oops.' He rubbed his jaw. 'I am so tired. I haven't slept.'

Come, I signed. *Lie here. In my bed.*

I jumped off the bed and tugged at Father's arm. He allowed me to guide him to the bed and settled back with a groan. I sat down in the visitor's chair.

'Thanks, sweetheart,' Father said softly, his eyes already heavy lidded. 'I . . . I'm sorry . . .'

I held up a hand to stop him. We were all sorry enough as it was, I didn't want any more apologizing for who did what when.

Father yawned. 'When I got to the hospital this afternoon, I stopped by to see your friend. You really ought to visit him.'

Friend? What friend?

Father smiled. 'Your friend . . . Danny.'

Danny! I'd totally forgotten about Danny. How many centuries ago was it that we'd revealed our real names to each other? How many millennia had passed since we decided to meet?

'He knows you're here. I told him you might drop by,' Father smiled. 'Go on. Danny's probably just as bored as you are. He's just around the corner. Room 214.'

There was a mirror in the hallway outside Room 214. I stared at myself. The nurses had not insisted that I wear a hospital gown. But still, I wasn't exactly in my best jeans and my T-shirt was old and faded.

Stop that, I told myself sternly. You're Stroppy-weather and don't you forget it.

The door was ajar. Cautiously I peeked in.

There on the bed was Danny sipping a glass of water.

It looked huge in his hands. The bed looked massive too. The pillows loomed like cliffs above his head. A plaster the size of a large white cream puff perched on his brow. His face was a peanut with huge jug ears and a forest of standing-up black hair. The nurses had taken away all his safety-pin piercings, his ripped jeans, his shoes. Above his head a bottle of colourless liquid drip-dripped down a thin hose cabled to his wrist.

When did Danny turn into this scrawny little thing in a hospital gown made for an elephant? When we were still bantering on the computer, I had imagined him taller, wider, with more meat on him.

I took one step into the room, then stopped, wondering if it was too late to turn round, run away.

He put the glass down on the side table. There was a twinkle in his eye. His hands began to sign, the tube pulling at the drip so hard I winced. But the hose was taped firmly enough to his wrist.

Wow! He winked at me. *This is like a BLIND DATE!*

Annoyance flared hot and pointy in my chest. The cheek!

You should be so LUCKY! I scowled, my hands throwing the words at him like darts.

He burst out laughing, his thin shoulders shaking under the voluminous hospital nightie.

What was so funny? I clenched my fists, a red fog descending on my head. Making contact with Danny on the Internet had been a mistake. Wanting to meet him had been a mistake. Visiting him here in the hospital was a gigantic, humongous mistake. What an idiot you've been, Rosa. Look at that moron. He's shown you up for a gullible, stupid fool!

I grabbed the glass of water on his night table and poured it over his head and down his chest. His braying stopped abruptly and he gazed with stupefied eyes at the spreading map of dampness on the sheet and gown.

I grinned. *Funny enough for you?* I signed.

He burst out laughing again, and this time I joined him – I couldn't help it; his laughter was so infectious, lighter than air. I'd never laughed like that before. Our laughter filled the room like a balloon, pushing out all our cares and worries and all the bad things that had gone by. We were buoyant, floaty things and we drifted up and up and up.

I thought we would never stop laughing, but we had to when a nurse marched in and lectured us about manners in the hospital and oh no, what happened to the sheets, and you young people should really know better.

And then she made Danny get out of bed while she changed the sheets. We stood side by side, watching – him next to the drip in a nightdress that revealed skinny, hairy legs, the tattooed snake peeking out at the collar, and me alongside with a hand over my mouth to stop the giggles. Two un-repentant naughty children.

No, it wasn't at all like a blind date.

More like a reunion of dear friends.

Danny refused to see anything weird about him stalking Father and me stalking him and us stalking each other.

I like your dad, he signed, shrugging. *I wanted to know more about him.*

Creepy! I signed back.

Crafty! he replied. *I like your dad. Honest!* And from the way those twinkly eyes suddenly looked so earnest, I knew he meant it.

When he found out that I was Doc's own daughter, Danny said, it felt like a fringe benefit. In fact, he used the word bonus, spelling it out with his fingers with such a smirk I almost emptied another glass of water over his head.

He confessed that he had been planning for our

first meeting long before I revealed my true location. It involved a picnic on the beach, a sunset, a box of chocolates, a shared flask of sweet milky tea, his camera on a tripod to capture the momentous occasion. I was blushing so hard I thought my cheeks would explode from the heat. I waited for him to snicker sarcastically, turn it all into a joke. But his eyes were big and sincere as a puppy's.

I'd spoiled all his plotting by insisting that we meet on the self-same evening. He sounded just like me. Excited and terrified and worried about his terrible Frankenstein secret. And what if I didn't like him, what if I screamed and stuck a pitchfork into him, what if he was too ugly, what if I was too good to be friends with him?

So he decided to stop at a bar at the edge of the village. Fortify himself with a little alcohol.

You drink? I signed, distaste in the curl of my lip.

That's the problem, he signed sheepishly. *I DON'T drink.*

He was ready with Plan A and Plan B in case the bartender refused to serve him because he was underage. But the barman didn't even give Danny a second glance. He just pulled the beer and took the money. Danny immediately retired to the darkest, most out of the way corner of the bar, the better to stay invisible.

And how was your beer? I signed.

He made a sour face. The beer tasted so foul he couldn't bear to take a second sip.

By that time it was pouring hard outside and the bar began to steam as it filled up with burly working men and tall teenagers dressed in sports sweats.

'Hey, the rain's stopped,' someone yelled. 'Here comes the sun!'

Everyone gave a loud cheer, even though Danny could see through the bar's clouded windows that it wasn't true, and anyway it was way past sundown. But the thought of the weather turning launched a ripple of banter up and down the crowd. They started joking about Mirasol's miserable weather. And then they were joking about ghosts. And then they were joking about all sorts of stupid supernatural creatures. Yaya would have felt totally at home.

And then someone shouted, *'Look out*, there are *monsters* about!' A bunch of boys pretended they had the Calm, pointing at their necks and groaning and staggering about and grunting with bulging eyes like the zombies from that Michael Jackson video. It got everyone else going, and suddenly the entire bar had turned into a scrum of sweating bodies, all pushing and shouting and raucous laughter.

It was friendly enough . . . but there was a dangerous, scary edge to it and Danny realized that he ought to get out before things went beyond good-natured.

But he was too late.

When he got up to push his way through the mêlée the play-fighting had already escalated into a hard shoving. Danny found himself sucked into the middle of a blind scuffle, men grunting and laughing as they grappled. He was caught in a vortex of hands pushing and pulling and grabbing and dragging.

And then his scarf was on the floor.

He dived to pick it up. Too late.

There were horrified shouts and bodies recoiled. The laughter in the room faltered as the men stepped away, forming a wide circle around Danny, their fists clenched.

Danny could smell their fear in that crowded room, sharp and pungent.

They set upon him.

'*Monster!*' the scrum panted in one voice. '*Monster!*' Someone's knuckle connected painfully with his eye. He tried to curl up into a ball, arms over his head, to give them less to kick, but even the most wildly aimed blows made painful contact. Two rugby types picked him up and swung him hard against the wall.

In the end he managed to lock himself in the bathroom. But when he climbed out the window they were waiting for him.

When he opened his eyes again, he was lying under a night sky, the rain spattering around him. He was lying in something thick and oozing. There was a putrid stench, like dead things mixed with lavatory unmentionables. He could feel tiny feet scampering about near his head. Giant cockroaches? Rats? He was so addled that it took him a while to figure out that he was lying in a large, open sewer. Then he remembered the brawl in the bar. And then he remembered that he was meant to meet me on the beach.

He dragged himself out of the muck and staggered his way to the promenade.

And when I was not there, he stumbled to our house.

Maybe those knocks he'd received on his skull had turned him stupid, or maybe he was confused by the darkness, or maybe he never had any good sense to start with – but the only thing on Danny's mind was that he had to turn up.

He didn't want me to think he was the sort of friend who would let me down.

34

The hospital only kept me for twenty-four hours and when they sent me home, I found that Father had launched an enquiry of his own. He drove all the way to Mirasol International to ask questions, double-checking the short report that the police had grudgingly given him. What time had Kat's flight arrived? What time did she call a cab? Could she have boarded a plane returning to London?

He got up in the wee hours to make calls to England, trying to find out more about Kat's life. Where did she live? Where did she work? Who were her friends?

'Doc, you are a medic, not a detective,' Yaya chided him. 'And you are definitely not getting rich making all those overseas calls!'

But Father just shrugged, saying, 'I need to know.'

Which was good. Because I needed to know too.

* * *

The broken, obsessed creature who had made Father and Mother's lives hell all those years ago was not the same person he discovered in his investigations.

After she deliberately took herself away from her sister, Kat had become a specialist nurse at a neurology hospital – and she was good at what she did. Her colleagues described her as efficient, sensible, unflappable. She had even won an innovation award for her excellent work.

She was well liked, had a large circle of friends and acquaintances that she saw regularly. She loved the cinema, one of her friends told Father. She even attended a film club. It formed a large part of her social life.

No, not a sad, crazy loner.

But then, over the past year, her friends noticed a change. She became quiet, suddenly secretive. She began missing film club meetings, stopped attending socials. At work, she became unreliable. Missed appointments. Turned up late for work.

And then she resigned from her job altogether – 'for personal reasons' her letter said.

It had taken her years to build the walls that kept the delusions at bay. But that piece about Father in the *Medical Journal* had undone her in an instant. Her delusions were back with a vengeance. Systematically she had telephoned every hospital in Mirasol until she found Father's clinic. After that, it hadn't been very hard to extract Father's home address from a hospital clerk too awed by the overseas phone call from London to resist.

And when she got the address, she didn't hesitate. She resigned from her job. Cancelled the lease to her flat in North London. Closed everything down. Put all her belongings into storage. Bought the plane ticket. Flew to Mirasol.

'So . . . where has she gone?' Yaya asked after Father told us the story, her voice brash in the hushed room.

'Well . . . the police think she's probably done what she did before, which was get herself as far away from us as possible, for her sake as well as ours. But she hasn't gone back. Nobody's heard from her. Her things are still in storage apparently.'

'It's good you do this investigation,' Yaya declared. 'Just in case she goes crazy again, comes back and does something terrible to you.'

Father folded his arms across his chest. Our eyes met. Yaya was right, it was entirely possible. But that wasn't why Father had gone through all the effort of finding out what Kat's life had been like.

'Oh, Doc. You are sad,' Yaya tutted. 'Rosa, look, he's sad.'

'I'm not sad,' Father said.

Yaya rolled her eyes. 'Yes, you are. You're sad about that crazy woman.'

'I . . . I . . . !' Father sputtered, glaring at Yaya. 'You wouldn't know how I feel. I'm not sad. Why should I be?'

But looking at him, what else but sadness could have cut those deep lines into his face and turned down the corners of his mouth?

I feel it too, Father. Somehow, we both lost something.

35

You stumble on the broken promenade. Your breath is coming in gasps and I can hear the *thump thump* of your heart. You've been running.

It's a beautiful day. The sky is high and not too wet, the sea is broad, the sand white and untrodden, and the mountain gazes greenly over everything like a contented matriarch at the end of a long family table.

Thump thump. Your heart is beating strong and fast. It reminds me of that time when we lay side by side on our shared bed, dreaming about the future.

You were talking up a storm, Kat! Building this massive, detailed fantasy of us living in adjoining houses, sharing one big garden where our children would mingle and play and some-times forget which mother belonged to whom. We would share a great big dining room, you said, and our families would always, always, sit together for every evening meal.

And then you stopped talking suddenly, covered your face. I was alarmed, but then you looked up, your eyes wet. 'I'm so excited,' you said. 'My heart is so full I'm afraid it might burst.'

And I put my hand over your heart and you put yours over mine and we listened to the drumming of each other's hearts.

You stand on the promenade, your eyes staring into the distance and it is only when I look more closely that I realize. Your sleeve is torn, your face bruised, and tears shine on your cheeks. Oh, Kat.

And then you smile.

Such a beautiful smile. It transforms your face. All the cares vanish instantly and a sparkle appears in your eyes. You whisper something and it's such a soft whisper I have to lean closer to hear.

You had a baby, you whisper. *A little girl. Rosa.*

And I can see now how full of gladness you are. You're happy for me. Happy that I had the life I'd wanted. Husband. Child. Home.

We'd spun that dream together, hadn't we? We were girls, hands entwined, imagining things in the moonlight.

Beautiful girl, you whisper to yourself. And in your eyes I see my Rosa, fresh-faced, open – the spitting image of us, Kat! Our girl, with all her tomorrows ahead of her.

Then a cloud dangles low and you look up at the sky, your eyes half closed against the soft wetness falling loosely from above.

Remember when Father used to take us to the beach? He waited until it was deserted, until all the holiday-makers had left, and then he would fetch us. And then we could dance and run and play on the sand to our heart's content.

You march to the far end of the promenade, with that old weather-beaten sign. Remember how Mother used to point it out to us, read it aloud in her most serious voice, remind us time and again. *Warning: Do not go far into the water.*

And how we laughed and teased, daring each other to go in, pushing one another towards the surf's froth.

You laugh out loud and stretch your arms wide as if you would embrace the entire width of the horizon.

And then you look straight at me.

Oh no, Kat. You mustn't.

I try to look away, try to break your gaze, but you wouldn't let me. You hold me with your eyes as you step quickly into the wet sand, hurrying, hurrying . . . striding into the water, deeper and deeper, the water washing gently around you.

No, Kat. Don't do it.

But you hold me tight with those eyes, determined and defiant.

No. Please.

Deeper and deeper you go. And soon you are beyond the line of safety, where the water loses its gentility and wraps itself around you, grasping, pulling, tugging.

You reach out.

No, I won't! I won't let you, Kat!

But when I feel your touch I can't help it.

I pull you close and we stand there with the sea tightening around us, your cheek against mine.

I pull back to stare into your dark eyes, afraid for you. But you just smile. And you reach round me to tug at my hair the way you used to when we were children.

It's OK, you whisper. It's going to be OK.

36

When Father announced over dinner one night that we were moving to London, Yaya gave a whoop and I swear she almost kissed Father she was so excited. It was her wish come true. How many times had she nagged Father to get me off Mirasol? How many times did Father and I have to sit through one of Yaya's 'what's best for Rosa' lectures?

Then she whirled round and ran up the stairs, taking the steps two at a time. I could hear things banging and her feet clattering back and forth on the wooden floor above our head.

'Doc, where is your old blue suitcase?' she yelled down the stairs.

She was *packing*?

But there was guilt in the look Father gave me.

'We should have done it a long time ago,' he said, his voice full of apology.

I just smiled. The truth was, I was expecting it.

After everything that had happened, leaving Mirasol was inevitable.

I climbed up to the attic, pushed the window open and knelt at the sill, my chin on my folded arms. The salty breeze blew gently, cooling the heat behind my eyelids.

It was already dark, of course, I could hear the sea panting on the shore and the hissing of the rain. A full moon coasted in and out of black cloud. Banawa's silhouette stared sightlessly at the heavens.

The rain stopped hissing.

I sat up. The yellow circle of moon hovered in the black sky, untroubled by cloud suddenly. It turned the sea from a black thing to a soft, glowing swell.

I half closed my eyes so that the shining lines of the ocean became a blur of glittery twinkles. The blur resolved into a wave of soft light. I squinted until the wave gathered itself into a pale oval face, with dark hints of eyes and gleaming lips that moved in sound-less whispers.

Mother, it was you, wasn't it? It was you on the beach.

The lips seemed to smile.

Mother, I'm sorry I ran from you. I was suddenly afraid. I wasn't ready. I guess it's one thing to want something and another to have it.

And now . . . well, we're leaving Mirasol. And I guess I should say goodbye but I can't.

I mean, goodbye means never being with you again, doesn't it? But how can that be? You're in every cell of my body. I can feel it. You are everywhere and in everything.

I can't do goodbye, sorry.

37

Every seat had a small monitor and we could watch the plane's progress as it set off, slowly lumbering towards the start of the runway. When we got there, I stared in disbelief at the airstrip stretching down, down into the ocean.

The plane seemed far too bulky to float in the sky. Inside, it felt cramped, everyone shuffling up against each other as we took our seats, bumping elbows and knees. I had that feeling again, of sitting in a swarming ant's nest. Will I ever get used to being around so many people?

Danny had been totally unsympathetic, of course.

> **People are easy. You will get used to it.**

> **But what's the point?**

What's the point of
what?

What's the point of
everything? Of you
and me even
bothering to chat
now I'm just going
to disappear to
another place.

Nobody's going to
disappear.

It was just like Danny to dismiss something as
momentous as his best friend vanishing for ever. He
was too busy being a comedian to realize the enormity
of what was about to happen.

> It's probably just as well we're going if you think it's HILARIOUS that we're NEVER going to SEE each other again.

I folded my arms across my chest. Poke fun at that, idiot boy.

> Sometimes hilariousness is the only defence.

> Oh, forget it.

I was so tired and so fed up I got up to go. But before I could snap the laptop closed, Danny sent a bubble flashing up on the screen.

> Don't you dare turn your laptop off.

I sat down again.

> I've only just found you. I was looking forward to . . . EVERYTHING.

> But hey, if MY parents suddenly said I had to move to a place where the Calm was not an excuse to beat a guy up, I'd be GLAD.

I stared at the screen, my heart beating painfully in my chest. So he wanted me to just go?

> Stroppy?

> Well excuse me while I get out of your life since you're just as happy when I'm not there.

Can't you read, Rosa? Do I have to spell it out?????????????? I'm GLAD.

Glad?

It's going to be a better life, dude, and you KNOW it!

Yeah?

Yeah! And hey, I'm still going to be here.

Here? Where exactly is here?

> **Right here in your computer. Your virtual friend.**

Oh, you're a funny one, aren't you, Danny? We'll be full circle, then. Back to just comments and likes and sharing photos and silly videos.

> **Right.**

> **It's not perfect, but it will do fine for now. I'm not letting you get rid of me so easily.**

I had to smile.

I could picture the wink, the lopsided grin, the unruly black hair, the safety pins in one eyebrow and on the tip of one of those jug ears. Danny was right, we still had cyberspace. The thought didn't make me feel any less lonely.

But it was a tiny comfort.

*　*　*

The plane revved its engine to a high-pitched whine. Just when the whine was becoming unbearable, the plane threw itself down the strip, racing towards the ocean.

I was surprised to find my teeth chattering; I was afraid to look into the monitor to watch the ocean rising to meet us.

I was also afraid to look out the window but I forced myself to look, if only to gaze into Banawa's wet, watching eyes for the last time. But we were on the wrong side. Banawa was looking away.

There was a loud *bang* and I would have leaped out of my chair had I not been belted down. 'It's just the plane retracting its wheels,' Father said, patting my knee.

The plane didn't fall into the sea. Instead, it flew up towards the sky, so steeply that it felt like we were lying on our backs, looking straight up into the sinister black cloud carpet above, rain streaking horizontally across the windows.

It punctured the cloud layer like a dart. One moment we were struggling blindly through the shapeless dark mass, the next we had burst out into a red and gold world, with a fat oblong sun on the horizon, sitting on a nest of white cloud like a giant yellow egg.

I felt Father's hand on mine and I realized I'd been clinging to the armrests so tightly that my knuckles shone white. With an effort, I let go.

'Are you all right?' he asked me gently.

'I'm OK,' Yaya said. She sat on the other side of me, her eyes shut tight, a rosary clutched to her breast.

Father looked anxiously at the tears on my cheeks but I smiled, trying to reassure him. Danny had said I would feel like this. Excited and sad at the same time.

I was looking forward to my new life, but I couldn't help feeling bereft. Mirasol was the only place I'd ever called home and I was going to miss it.

The plane circled, the wing on my side dipping towards the earth. Suddenly we were looking down, down into Banawa's green face. From above, the water didn't stream from her eyes but down the side of her face. This is the last time I will see Banawa, I thought, and she isn't weeping.

And then I couldn't see her any more because the plane tilted up and we flew straight into a fierce light.

This must be what it's like to be born.

First, there you are in the darkness of your mother's womb, not knowing anything and not wanting anything to change.

And then suddenly you are out, naked and starving hungry in a shining new world.

What's up, Danny?

Nothing much. How about you, Strop? What's up?

Everything.

Everything?

Yup. Everything.

Everything, wow. Well, that's just wonderful, dude.

It certainly is. And don't call me dude.

Thank you

In the acknowledgments of my last book, I ungratefully forgot to thank Sara Grant and Sara 'Slasher' O'Connor, founding sisters of the *Undiscovered Voices* anthology, who carefully sat me in the publishing roller coaster – then pushed.

To the original Stroppy, Anne Rooney of www.stroppyauthor.blogspot.com – for giving me permission to adapt her excellent screen name.

To Susan Quimpo, for telling me the original, true story of the double murder ghost.

To William Wymark Jacobs, with respect and gratitude, for writing the unforgettable scary story of my childhood, *The Monkey's Paw*.

To Ray Bradbury, whose short story *All Summer in a Day* inspired the idea of a distant place where the rain never stops falling.

To my editors: Simon Mason who told me to focus on what's great about my text, Bella Pearson, who sorted out my exposition of never letting go, and to

David Fickling, who wouldn't publish and let me be damned.

To David Deane, for another brilliant cover.

To my agent Hilary Delamere.

To the North London cafés and their kindly staff who let me sit for hours on their premises nursing decaffeinated coffee beyond redemption. Especially Caffe Nero, probably the best decaffeinated coffee in the world.

To all my writing friends who cheered me through my ever-changing text-in-progress.

To Mia, Jack, Nick and Richard. How lucky I am.

TALL STORY BY CANDY GOURLAY

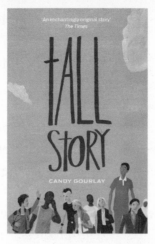

**What you want is not always what you get.
Even when your wishes come true.**

Andi desperately hopes her long lost half-brother Bernardo
will be as mad on basketball as she is. But when he steps off
the plane from the Philippines, she can't believe her eyes.
She hasn't seen him for ten years, but even so, how did he
get to be EIGHT FOOT TALL?

But Bernardo is not what he seems.
Bernardo is a hero, Bernardo works miracles,
and Bernardo has an amazing story to tell.

Tall Story is a bittersweet story, funny, sad, and magical.

'Charming' **Carousel**

'An uplifting and heart-warming tale - a real slam dunk!'
tbk magazine